The Influence of Old Norse Literature on English Literature

Conrad Hjalmar Nordby

Contents

THE INFLUENCE OF OLD NORSE

LITERATURE ON ENGLISH LITERATURE

BY

Conrad Hjalmar Nordby

THE INFLUENCE OF OLD NORSE LITERATURE

UPON ENGLISH LITERATURE

by

CONRAD HJALMAR NORDBY

1901

Deyr fe
deyja fraendr,
deyr sialfr it sama;
en orethstirr
deyr aldrigi
hveim er ser goethan getr.
Havamal, 75.

Cattle die,
kindred die,
we ourselves also die;
but the fair fame
never dies
of him who has earned it.

Thorpe's *Edda*.

PREFATORY NOTE.

The present publication is the only literary work left by its author. Unfortunately it lacks a few pages which, as his manuscript shows, he intended to add, and it also failed to receive his final revision. His friends have nevertheless deemed it expedient to publish the result of his studies conducted with so much ardor, in order that some memorial of his life and work should remain for the wider public. To those acquainted with him, no written words can represent the charm of his personality or give anything approaching an adequate impression of his ability and strength of character.

Conrad Hjalmar Nordby was born September 20, 1867, at Christiania, Norway. At the age of four he was brought to New York, where he was educated in the public schools. He was graduated from the College of the City of New York in 1886. From December of that year to June, 1893, he taught in Grammar School No. 55, and in September, 1893, he was called to his Alma Mater as Tutor in English. He was promoted to the rank of Instructor in 1897, a position which he held at the time of his death. He died in St. Luke's Hospital, October 28, 1900. In October, 1894, he began his studies in the School of Philosophy of Columbia University, taking courses in Philosophy and Education under Professor Nicholas Murray Butler, and in Germanic Literatures and Germanic Philology under Professors Boyesen, William H. Carpenter and Calvin Thomas. It was under the guidance of Professor Carpenter that the present work was conceived and executed.

Such a brief outline of Mr. Nordby's career can, however, give but an imperfect view of his activities, while it gives none at all of his influence. He was a teacher who impressed his personality, not only upon his students, but upon all who knew him. In his character were united force and refinement, firmness and geniality. In his earnest work with his pupils, in his lectures to the teachers of the New York Public Schools and to other audiences, in his personal influence upon all with whom he came in contact, he spread the taste for beauty, both of poetry and of life. When his body was carried to the grave, the grief was not confined to a few intimate friends; all who had known him felt that something noble and beautiful had vanished from their lives.

In this regard his career was, indeed, rich in achievement, but when we consider what, with his large equipment, he might have done in the world of scholarship, the promise, so untimely blighted, seems even richer. From early youth he had been a true lover of books. To him they were not dead things; they palpitated with the life blood of master spirits. The enthusiasm for William Morris displayed in the present essay is typical of his feeling for all that he considered best in literature. Such an enthusiasm, communicated to those about him, rendered him a vital force in every company where works of creative genius could be a theme of conversation.

A love of nature and of art accompanied and reinforced this love of literature; and all combined to produce the effect of wholesome purity and elevation which continually emanated from him. His influence, in fact, was largely of that pervasive sort which depends, not on any special word uttered, and above all, not on any preachment, but upon the entire character and life of the man. It was for this reason that his modesty never concealed his strength. He shrunk above all things from pushing himself forward and demanding public notice, and yet few ever met him without feeling the force of character that lay behind his gentle and almost retiring demeanor. It was easy to recognize that here was a man, self-centered and whole.

In a discourse pronounced at a memorial meeting, the Rev. John Coleman Adams justly said: "If I wished to set before my boy a type of what is best and most lovable in the American youth, I think I could find no more admirable character than that of Conrad Hjalmar Nordby. A young man of the people, with all their unexhausted force, vitality and enthusiasm; a man of simple aims and honest ways; as chivalrous and high-minded as any knight of old; as pure in life as a woman; at once gentle and brave, strong and sweet, just and loving; upright, but no Pharisee; earnest, but never sanctimonious; who took his work as a pleasure, and his pleasure as an innocent joy; a friend to be coveted; a disciple such as the Saviour must have loved; a true son of God, who dwelt in the Father's house. Of such youth our land may well be proud; and no man need speak despairingly of a nation whose life and institutions can ripen such a fruit."

L.F.M.
COLLEGE OF THE CITY OF NEW YORK,
May 15, 1901.

INTRODUCTORY.

It should not be hard for the general reader to understand that the influence which is the theme of this dissertation is real and explicable. If he will but call the roll of his favorite heroes, he will find Sigurd there. In his gallery of wondrous women, he certainly cherishes Brynhild. These poetic creations belong to the English-speaking race, because they belong to the world. And if one will but recall the close kinship of the Icelandic and the Anglo-Saxon languages, he will not find it strange that the spirit of the old Norse sagas lives again in our English song and story.

The survey that this essay takes begins with Thomas Gray (1716-1771), and comes down to the present day. It finds the fullest measure of the old Norse poetic spirit in William Morris (1834-1896), and an increasing interest and delight in it as we come toward our own time. The enterprise of learned societies and enlightened book publishers has spread a knowledge of Icelandic literature among the reading classes of the present day; but the taste for it is not to be accounted for in the same way. That is of nobler birth than of erudition or commercial pride. Is it not another expression of that changed feeling for the things that pertain to the common people, which distinguishes our century from the last? The historian no longer limits his study to camp and court; the poet deigns to leave the drawing-room and library for humbler scenes. Folk-lore is now dignified into a science. The touch of nature has made the whole world kin, and our highly civilized century is moved by the records of the passions of the earlier society.

This change in taste was long in coming, and the emotional phase of it has preceded the intellectual. It is interesting to note that Gray and Morris both failed to carry their public with them all the way. Gray, the most cultured man of his time, produced art forms totally different from those in vogue, and Walpole[1] said of these forms: "Gray has added to his poems three ancient odes from Norway and Wales ... they are not interesting, and do not, like his other poems, touch any passion.... Who can care through what horrors a Runic savage arrived at all the joys and glories they could conceive--the supreme felicity of boozing ale out of the skull of an enemy in Odin's Hall?"

Morris, the most versatile man of his time, found plenty of praise for his art work, until he preached social reform to Englishmen. Thereafter the art of William Morris was not so highly esteemed, and the best poet in England failed to attain the laurel on the death of Tennyson.

Of this change of taste more will be said as this essay is developed. These introductory words must not be left, however, without an explanation of the word "Influence," as it is used in the subject-title. This paper will not undertake to prove that the course of English literature was diverted into new channels by the introduction of Old Norse elements, or that its nature was materially changed thereby. We find an expression and a justification of our present purpose in Richard Price's Preface to the 1824 edition of Warton's "History of English Poetry" (p. 15): "It was of importance to notice the successive acquisitions, in the shape of translation or imitation, from the more polished productions of Greece and Rome; and to mark the dawn of that aera, which, by directing the human mind to the study of classical antiquity, was to give a new impetus to science and literature, and by the changes it introduced to effect a total revolution in the laws which had previously governed them." Were Warton writing his history to-day, he would have to account for later eras as well as for the Elizabethan, and the method would be the same. How far the Old Norse literature has helped to form these later eras it is not easy to say, but the contributions may be counted up, and their literary value noted. These are the commission of the present essay. When the record is finished, we shall be in possession of information that may account for certain considerable writers of our day, and certain tendencies of thought.

I.
THE BODY OF OLD NORSE LITERATURE.

First, let us understand what the Old Norse literature was that has been sending out this constantly increasing influence into the world of poetry.

It was in the last four decades of the ninth century of our era that Norsemen began to leave their own country and set up new homes in Iceland. The sixty years ending with 930 A.D. were devoted to taking up the land, and the hundred years that ensued after that date were devoted to quarreling about that land. These quarrels were the origin of the Icelandic family sagas. The year 1000 brought Christianity to the island, and the period from 1030 to 1120 were years of peace in which stories of the former time passed from mouth to mouth. The next century saw these stories take written form, and the period from 1220 to 1260 was the golden age of this literature. In 1264, Iceland passed under the rule of Norway, and a decline of literature began, extending until 1400, the end of literary production in Iceland. In the main, the authors of Iceland are unknown[2].

There are several well-marked periods, therefore, in Icelandic literary production. The earliest was devoted to poetry, Icelandic being no different from most other languages in the precedence of that form. Before the settlement of Iceland, the Norse lands were acquainted with songs about gods and champions, written in a simple verse form. The first settlers wrote down some of these, and forgot others. In the **Codex Regius**, preserved in the Royal Library in Copenhagen, we have a collection of these songs. This material was published in the seventeenth century as the **Saemundar Edda**, and came to be known as the

Elder or *Poetic Edda*. Both titles are misnomers, for Saemund had nothing to do with the making of the book, and *Edda* is a name belonging to a book of later date and different purpose.

This work--not a product of the soil as folk-songs are--is the fountain head of Old Norse mythology, and of Old Norse heroic legends. *Voeluspa* and *Havamal* are in this collection, and other songs that tell of Odin and Baldur and Loki. The Helgi poems and the Voelsung poems in their earliest forms are also here.

A second class of poetry in this ancient literature is that called "Skaldic." Some of this deals with mythical material, and some with historical material. A few of the skalds are known to us by name, because their lives were written down in later sagas. Egill Skallagrimsson, known to all readers of English and Scotch antiquities, Eyvind Skaldaspillir and Sigvat are of this group.

Poetic material that is very rich is found in Snorri Sturluson's work on Old Norse poetics, entitled *The Edda*, and often referred to as the *Younger* or *Prose Edda*.

More valuable than the poetry is the prose of this literature, especially the *Sagas*. The saga is a prose epic, characteristic of the Norse countries. It records the life of a hero, told according to fixed rules. As we have said, the sagas were based upon careers run in Iceland's stormy time. They are both mythical and historical. In the mythical group are, among others, the *Voelsunga Saga*, the *Hervarar Saga*, *Frieththjofs Saga* and *Ragnar Loethbroks Saga*. In the historical group, the flowering time of which was 1200-1270, we find, for example, *Egils Saga*, *Eyrbyggja Saga*, *Laxdaela Saga*, *Grettis Saga*, *Njals Saga*. A branch of the historic sagas is the Kings' Sagas, in which we find *Heimskringla*, the *Saga of Olaf Tryggvason*, the *Flatey Book*, and others.

This sketch does not pretend to indicate the quantity of Old Norse literature. An idea of that is obtained by considering the fact that eleven columns of the ninth edition of the ***Encyclopaedia Britannica*** are devoted to recording the works of that body of writings.

II.

THROUGH THE MEDIUM OF LATIN.

THOMAS GRAY (1716-1771).

In the eighteenth century, Old Norse literature was the lore of antiquarians. That it is not so to-day among English readers is due to a line of writers, first of whom was Thomas Gray. In the thin volume of his poetry, two pieces bear the sub-title: "An Ode. From the Norse Tongue." These are "The Fatal Sisters," and "The Descent of Odin," both written in 1761, though not published until 1768. These poems are among the latest that Gray gave to the world, and are interesting aside from our present purpose because they mark the limit of Gray's progress toward Romanticism.

We are not accustomed to think of Gray as a Romantic poet, although we know well that the movement away from the so-called Classicism was begun long before he died. The Romantic element in his poetry is not obvious; only the close observer detects it, and then only in a few of the poems.

The Pindaric odes exhibit a treatment that is Romantic, and the Norse and Welsh adaptations are on subjects that are Romantic. But we must go to his letters to find proof positive of his sympathy with the breaking away from Classicism. Here are records of a love of outdoors that reveled in mountain-climbing and the buffeting of storms. Here are appreciations of Shakespeare and of Milton, the like of which were not often proclaimed in his generation. Here is ecstatic admiration of ballads and of the Ossian imitations, all so unfashionable in the literary culture of the day. While dates disprove Lowell's statement in his essay on Gray that "those anti-classical yearnings of Gray began after he had ceased producing," it is certain that very little of his poetic work expressed these yearnings. "Elegance, sweetness, pathos, or even majesty he could achieve, but never that force which vibrates in every verse of larger moulded men." Change Lowell's word "could" to "did," and this sentence will serve our purpose here.

Our interest in Gray's Romanticism must confine itself to the two odes from the Old Norse. It is to be noted that the first transplanting to English poetry of Old Norse song came about through the scholar's agency, not the poet's. It was Gray, the scholar, that made "The Descent of Odin" and "The Fatal Sisters." They were intended to serve as specimens of a forgotten literature in a history of English poetry. In the "Advertisement" to "The Fatal Sisters" he tells how he came to give up the plan: "The Author has long since drop'd his design, especially after he heard, that it was already in the hands of a Person well qualified to do it justice, both by his taste, and his researches into antiquity." Thomas Warton's *History of English Poetry* was the execution of this design, but in that book no place was found for these poems.

In his absurd *Life of Gray*, Dr. Johnson said: "His translations of Northern and Welsh Poetry deserve praise: the imagery is preserved, perhaps often improved, but the language is unlike the language of other poets." There are more correct statements in this sentence, perhaps, than in any other in the essay, but this is because ignorance sometimes hits the truth. It is not likely that the poems would have been understood without the preface and the explanatory notes, and these, in a measure, made the reader interested in the literature from which they were drawn. Gray called the pieces "dreadful songs," and so in very truth they are. Strength is the dominant note, rude, barbaric strength, and only the art of Gray saved it from condemnation. To-day, with so many imitations from Old Norse to draw upon, we cannot point to a single poem which preserves spirit and form as well as those of Gray. Take the stanza:

> Horror covers all the heath,
> Clouds of carnage blot the sun,
> Sisters, weave the web of death;
> Sisters, cease, the work is done.

The strophe is perfect in every detail. Short lines, each ending a sentence; alliteration; words that echo the sense, and just four strokes to paint a picture which has an atmosphere that whisks you into its own world incontinently. It is no wonder that writers of later days who have tried similar imitations ascribe to Thomas Gray the mastership.

That this poet of the eighteenth century, who "equally despised what was Greek and what was Gothic," should have entered so fully into the spirit and letter of Old Norse poetry is little short of marvelous. If Professor G.L. Kittredge had not gone so minutely into the question of Gray's knowledge of Old Norse,[3] we might be pardoned for still believing with Gosse[4] that the poet learned Icelandic in his later life. Even after reading Professor Kittredge's essay, we cannot understand how Gray could catch the metrical lilt of the Old Norse with only a Latin version to transliterate the parallel Icelandic. We suspect that Gray's knowledge was fuller than Professor Kittredge will allow, although we must admit that superficial knowledge may coexist with a fine interpretative spirit. Matthew Arnold's knowledge of Celtic literature was meagre, yet he wrote memorably and beautifully on that subject, as Celts themselves will acknowledge.[5]

THE SOURCES OF GRAY'S KNOWLEDGE.

It has already been said that only antiquarians had knowledge of things Icelandic in Gray's time. Most of this knowledge was in Latin, of course, in ponderous tomes with wonderful, long titles; and the list of them is awe-inspiring. In all likelihood Gray did not use them all, but he met references to them in the books he did consult. Professor Kittredge mentions them in the paper already quoted, but they are here arranged in the order of publication, and the list is lengthened to include some books that were inspired by the interest in Gray's experiments.

=1636= and =1651=. Wormius. *Seu Danica literatura antiquissima, vulgo Gothica dicta, luci reddita opera Olai Wormii. Cui accessit de prisca Danorum Poesi Dissertatio.* Hafniae. 1636. Edit. II. 1651.

The essay on poetry contains interlinear Latin translations of the *Epicedium* of Ragnar Loethbrok, and of the *Drapa* of Egill Skallagrimsson. Bound with the second edition of 1651, and bearing the date 1650, is: *Specimen Lexici runici, obscuriorum quarundam vocum, quae*
in priscis occurrunt historiis et poetis Danicis enodationem exhibens. Collectum a Magno Olavio pastore Laufasiensi, ... nunc in ordinem redactum, auctum et locupletatum ab Olao Wormio. Hafniae.

This glossary adduces illustrations from the great poems of Icelandic literature. Thus early the names and forms of the ancient literature were known.

=1665.= Resenius. *Edda Islandorum an. Chr. MCCXV islandice conscripta per Snorronem Sturlae Islandiae. Nomophylacem nunc primum islandice, danice et latine ... Petri Johannis Resenii* ... Havniae. 1665.

A second part contains a disquisition on the philosophy of the *Voeluspa* and the *Havamal*.

=1670.= Sheringham. *De Anglorum Gentis Origine Disceptatio. Qua eorum migrationes, variae sedes, et ex parte res gestae, a confusione Linguarum, et dispersione Gentium, usque ad adventum eorum in Britanniam investigantur; quaedam de veterum Anglorum religione, Deorum cultu, eorumque opinionibus de statu animae post hanc vitam, explicantur. Authore* Roberto Sheringhamo. Cantabrigiae. 1670.

Chapter XII contains an account of Odin extracted from the *Edda*, Snorri Sturluson and others.

=1679-92.= Temple. Two essays: "Of Heroic Virtue," "Of Poetry," contained in The Works of Sir William Temple. London. 1757. Vol. 3, pp. 304-429.

=1689.= Bartholinus. *Thomae Bartholini Antiquitatum Danicarum de causis contemptae a Danis adhuc gentilibus mortis libri III ex vetustis codicibus et monumentis hactenus ineditis congestae.* Hafniae. 1689.

The pages of this book are filled, with extracts from Old Norse sagas and poetry which are translated into Latin. No student of the book could fail to get a considerable knowledge of the spirit and the form of the ancient literature.

=1691.= Verelius. *Index linguae veteris Scytho-Scandicae sive Gothicae ex vetusti aevi monumentis ... ed Rudbeck.* Upsalae. 1691.

=1697=. Torfaeus. *Orcades, seu rerum Orcadensium historiae*. Havniae. 1697.

=1697=. Perinskjoeld. *Heimskringla, eller Snorre Sturlusons Nordlaendske Konunga Sagor*. Stockholmiae. 1697.

Contains Latin and Swedish translation.

=1705=. Hickes. *Linguarum Vett. Septentrionalium thesaurus grammatico criticus et archaeologicus*. Oxoniae. 1703-5.

This work is discussed later.

=1716=. Dryden. *Miscellany Poems. Containing Variety of New Translations of the Ancient Poets*.... Published by Mr. Dryden. London. 1716.

=1720=. Keysler. *Antiquitates selectae septentrionales et Celticae quibus plurima loca conciliorum et capitularium explanantur, dogmata theologiae ethnicae Celtarum gentiumque septentrionalium cum moribus et institutis maiorum nostrorum circa idola, aras, oracula, templa, lucos, sacerdotes, regum electiones, comitia et monumenta sepulchralia una cum reliquiis gentilismi in coetibus christianorum ex monumentis potissimum hactenus ineditis fuse perquiruntur. Autore* Joh. Georgio Keysler. Hannoverae. 1720.

=1755=. Mallet. *Introduction a l'Histoire de Dannemarc ou l'on traite de la Religion, des Lois, des Moeurs, et des Usages des Anciens Danois. Par* M. Mallet. Copenhague. 1755.

Discussed later.

=1756=. Mallet. *Monumens de la Mythologie et la Poesie des Celtes et particulierement des anciens Scandinaves ... Par* M. Mallet. Copenhague. 1756.

=1763=. Percy. *Five Pieces of Runic Poetry translated from the Islandic Language*. London. 1763.

This book is described on a later page.

=1763=. Blair. *A Critical Dissertation on the Poems of Ossian, the Son of Fingal*. [By Hugh Blair.] London. 1763.

=1770=. Percy. *Northern Antiquities: or a description of the Manners, Customs, Religion and Laws of the ancient Danes, and other Northern Nations; including these of our own Saxon Ancestors. With a translation of the Edda or System of Runic Mythology, and other Pieces from the Ancient Icelandic Tongue. Translated from M. Mallet's Introduction a l'Histoire de Dannemarc*. London. 1770.

=1774=. Warton. *The History of English Poetry*. By Thomas Warton. London. 1774-81.

In this book the prefatory essay entitled "On the Origin of Romantic Fiction in Europe" is significant. It is treated at length later on.

SIR WILLIAM TEMPLE (1628-1699).

From the above list it appears that the earliest mention in the English language of Icelandic literature was Sir William Temple's. The two essays noted above have many references to Northern customs and songs. Macaulay's praise of Temple's style is well deserved, and the slighting remarks about the matter do not apply to the passages in evidence here. Temple's acknowledgments to Wormius indicate the source of his information, and it is a commentary upon the exactness of the antiquarian's knowledge that so many of the statements in Temple's essays are perfectly good to-day. Of course the terms "Runic" and "Gothic" were misused, but so were they a century later. Odin is "the first and great hero of the western Scythians; he led a mighty swarm of the Getes, under the name of Goths, from the Asiatic Scythia into the farthest northwest parts of Europe; he seated and spread his kingdom round the whole Baltic sea, and over all the islands in it, and extended

it westward to the ocean and southward to the Elve."[6] Temple places
Odin's expedition at two thousand years before his own time, but he gets
many other facts right. Take this summing up of the old Norse belief as
an example:

"An opinion was fixed and general among them, that death was but the
entrance into another life; that all men who lived lazy and inactive
lives, and died natural deaths, by sickness, or by age, went into vast
caves under ground, all dark and miry, full of noisom creatures, usual
in such places, and there forever grovelled in endless stench and
misery. On the contrary, all who gave themselves to warlike actions and
enterprises, to the conquests of their neighbors, and slaughters of
enemies, and died in battle, or of violent deaths upon bold adventures
or resolutions, they went immediately to the vast hall or palace of
Odin, their god of war, who eternally kept open house for all such
guests, where they were entertained at infinite tables, in perpetual
feasts and mirth, carousing every man in bowls made of the skulls of
their enemies they had slain, according to which numbers, every one in
these mansions of pleasure was the most honoured and the best
entertained."[7]

Thus before Gray was born, Temple had written intelligently in English
of the salient features of the Old Norse mythology. Later in the same
essay, he recognized that some of the civil and political procedures of
his country were traceable to the Northmen, and, what is more to our
immediate purpose, he recognized the poetic value of Old Norse song. On
p. 358 occurs this paragraph:

"I am deceived, if in this sonnet (two stanzas of 'Regner Lodbrog'), and
a following ode of Scallogrim there be not a vein truly poetical, and in
its kind Pindaric, taking it with the allowance of the different
climates, fashions, opinions, and languages of such distant countries."

Temple certainly had no knowledge of Old Norse, and yet, in 1679, he could write so of a poem which he had to read through the Latin. Sir William had a wide knowledge and a fine appreciation of literature, and an enthusiasm for its dissemination. He takes evident delight in telling the fact that princes and kings of the olden time did high honor to bards. He regrets that classic culture was snuffed out by a barbarous people, but he rejoices that a new kind came to take its place. "Some of it wanted not the true spirit of poetry in some degree, or that natural inspiration which has been said to arise from some spark of poetical fire wherewith particular men are born; and such as it was, it served the turn, not only to please, but even to charm, the ignorant and barbarous vulgar, where it was in use."[8]

It is proverbial that music hath charms to soothe the savage breast. That savage music charms cultivated minds is not proverbial, but it is nevertheless true. Here is Sir William Temple, scion of a cultured race, bearing witness to the fact, and here is Gray, a life-long dweller in a staid English university, endorsing it a half century later. As has been intimated, this was unusual in the time in which they lived, when, in Lowell's phrase, the "blight of propriety" was on all poetry. But it was only the rude and savage in an unfamiliar literature that could give pause in the age of Pope. The milder aspects of Old Norse song and saga must await the stronger century to give them favor. "Behold, there was a swarm of bees and honey in the carcass of the lion."

GEORGE HICKES (1642-1715).

The next book in the list that contains an English contribution to the knowledge of our subject is the *Thesaurus* of George Hickes. On p. 193 of Part I, there is a prose translation of "The Awakening of Angantyr," from the *Harvarar Saga*. Acknowledgment is given to Verelius for the text of the poem, but Hickes seems to have chosen this poem as the gem of the Saga. The translation is another proof of an antiquarian's taste and judgment, and the reader does not wonder that it soon found a wider audience through another publication. It was reprinted in the books of 1716 and 1770 in the above list. An extract or two will show that the vigor of the old poem has not been altogether lost in the translation:

Hervor.--Awake Angantyr, Hervor the only daughter of thee and Suafu doth awaken thee. Give me out of the tombe, the hardned[9] sword, which the dwarfs made for Suafurlama. Hervardur, Hiorvardur, Hrani, and Angantyr, with helmet, and coat of mail, and a sharp sword, with sheild and accoutrements, and bloody spear, I wake you all, under the roots of trees. Are the sons of Andgrym, who delighted in mischief, now become dust and ashes, can none of Eyvors sons now speak with me out of the habitations of the dead! Harvardur, Hiorvardur! so may you all be within your ribs, as a thing that is hanged up to putrifie among insects, unlesse you deliver me the sword which the dwarfs made ... and the glorious belt.

Angantyr.--Daughter Hervor, full of spells to raise the dead, why dost thou call so? wilt thou run on to thy own mischief? thou art mad, and out of thy senses, who art desperatly resolved to waken dead men. I was not buried either by father or other freinds. Two which lived after me got Tirfing, one of whome is now possessor thereof.

Hervor.--Thou dost not tell the truth: so let Odin hide thee in the tombe, as thou hast Tirfing by thee. Art thou unwilling, Angantyr, to give an inheritance to thy only child?...

Angantyr.--Fals woman, thou dost not understand, that thou speakest foolishly of that, in which thou dost rejoice, for Tirfing shall, if thou wilt beleive me, maid, destroy all thy offspring.

Hervor.--I must go to my seamen, here I have no mind to stay longer.

Little do I care, O Royall friend, what my sons hereafter quarrell about.

Angantyr.--Take and keep Hialmars bane, which thou shalt long have and enjoy, touch but the edges of it, there is poyson in both of them, it is a most cruell devourer of men.

Hervor.--I shall keep, and take in hand, the sharp sword which thou hast let me have: I do not fear, O slain father! what my sons hereafter may quarrell about.... Dwell all of you safe in the tombe, I must be gon, and hasten hence, for I seem to be, in the midst of a place where fire burns round about me.

One can well understand, who handles the ponderous *Thesaurus*, why the first English lovers of Old Norse were antiquarians. "The Awakening of Angantyr" is literally buried in this work, and only the student of Anglo-Saxon prosody would come upon it unassisted, since it is an illustration in a chapter of the *Grammaticae Anglo-Saxonicae et Moeso-Gothicae*. Students will remember in this connection that it was a work on poetics that saved for us the original Icelandic *Edda*. The Icelandic skald had to know his nation's mythology.

THOMAS PERCY (1729-1811).

The title of Chapter XXIII in Hickes' work indicates that even among learned doctors mistaken notions existed as to the relationship of the Teutonic languages. It took more than a hundred years to set the error right, but in the meanwhile the literature of Iceland was becoming better known to English readers. To the French scholar, Paul Henri Mallet (1730-1807), Europe owes the first popular presentation of Northern antiquities and literature. Appointed professor of belles-lettres in the Copenhagen academy he found himself with more time than students on his hands, because not many Danes at that time understood French. His leisure time was applied to the study of the antiquities of his adopted country, the King's commission for a history of Denmark making that necessary. As a preface to this work he published, in 1755, an ***Introduction a l'Histoire de Dannemarc ou l'on traite de la Religion, des Lois, des Moeurs et des Usages des Anciens Danois***, and, in 1756, the work in the list on a previous page. In this second book was the first translation into a modern tongue of the ***Edda***, and this volume, in consequence, attracted much attention. The great English antiquarian, Thomas Percy, afterward Bishop of Dromore, was early drawn to this work, and with the aid of friends he accomplished a translation of it, which was published in 1770.

Mallet's work was very bad in its account of the racial affinities of the nations commonly referred to as the barbarians that overturned the Roman empire and culture. Percy, who had failed to edit the ballad MSS. so as to please Ritson, was wise enough to see Mallet's error, and to insist that Celtic and Gothic antiquities must not be confounded. Mallet's translation of the ***Edda*** was imperfect, too, because he had followed the Latin version of Resenius, which was notoriously poor. Percy's ***Edda*** was no better, because it was only an English version of Mallet. But we are not concerned with these critical considerations here; and so it will be enough to record the fact that with the publication of Percy's ***Northern Antiquities***--the English name of Mallet's work--in 1770, knowledge of Icelandic literature passed from the exclusive control of learned antiquarians. More and more, as time went on, men went to the Icelandic originals, and translations of poems and sagas came from the press in increasing numbers. In the course of time came original works that were inspired by Old Norse stories and Old Norse conceptions.

We have already noted that Gray's poems on Icelandic themes, though written in 1761, were not published until 1768. Another delayed work on similar themes was Percy's ***Five Pieces of Runic Poetry***, which, the author tells us, was prepared for the press in 1761, but, through an accident, was not published until 1763. The preface has this interesting sentence: "It would be as vain to deny, as it is perhaps impolitic to mention, that this attempt is owing to the success of the Erse fragments." The book has an appendix containing the Icelandic originals of the poems translated, and that portion of the book shows that a scholar's hand and interest made the volume. So, too, does the close of the preface: "That the study of ancient northern literature hath its important uses has been often evinced by able writers: and that it is not dry or unamusive this little work it is hoped will demonstrate. Its aim at least is to shew, that if those kind of studies are not always employed on works of taste or classic elegance, they serve at least to unlock the treasures of native genius; they present us with frequent sallies of bold imagination, and constantly afford matter for philosophical reflection by showing the workings of the human mind in its almost original state of nature."

That original state was certainly one of original sin, if these poems are to be believed. Every page in this volume is drenched with blood, and from this book, as from Gray's poems and the other Old Norse imitations of the time, a picture of fierceness and fearfulness was the only one possible. Percy intimates in his preface that Icelandic poetry has other tales to tell besides the "Incantation of Hervor," the "Dying Ode of Regner Lodbrog," the "Ransome of Egill the Scald," and the "Funeral Song of Hacon," which are here set down; he offers the "Complaint of Harold" as a slight indication that the old poets left "behind them many pieces on the gentler subjects of love or friendship." But the time had not come for the presentation of those pieces.

All of these translations were from the Latin versions extant in Percy's time. This volume copied Hickes's translation of "Hervor's Incantation" modified in a few particulars, and like that one, the other translations in this volume were in prose. The work is done as well as possible, and it remained for later scholars to point out errors in translation. The negative contractions in Icelandic were as yet unfamiliar, and so, as Walter Scott pointed out (in *Edin. Rev.*, Oct., 1806), Percy made Regner Lodbrog say, "The pleasure of that day (of battle, p. 34 in this *Five Pieces*) was like having a fair virgin placed beside one in the bed," and "The pleasure of that day was like kissing a young widow at the highest seat of the table," when the poet really made the contrary statement.

Of course, the value of this book depends upon the view that is taken of it. Intrinsically, as literature, it is well-nigh valueless. It indicates to us, however, a constantly growing interest in the literature it reveals, and it undoubtedly directed the attention of the poets of the succeeding generation to a field rich in romantic possibilities. That no great work was then created out of this material was not due to neglect. As we shall see, many puny poets strove to breathe life into these bones, but the divine power was not in the poets. Some who were not poets had yet the insight to feel the value of this ancient literature, and they made known the facts concerning it. It seems a mechanical and unpromising way to have great poetry written, this calling out, "New Lamps for Old." Yet it is on record that great poems have been written at just such instigation.

THOMAS WARTON (1728-1790).

Historians[10] of Romanticism have marked Warton's *History of English Poetry* as one of the forces that made for the new idea in literature. This record of a past which, though out of favor, was immeasurably superior to the time of its historian, spread new views concerning the poetic art among the rising generation, and suggested new subjects as well as new treatments of old subjects. We have mentioned the fact that Gray handed over to Warton his notes for a contemplated history of poetry, and that Warton found no place in his work for Gray's adaptations from the Old Norse. Warton was not blind to the beauties of Gray's poems, nor did he fail to appreciate the merits of the literature which they illustrated. His scheme relegated his remarks concerning that poetry to the introductory dissertation, "Of the Origin of Romantic Fiction in Europe." What he had to say was in support of a theory which is not accepted to-day, and of course his statements concerning the origin of the Scandinavian people were as wrong as those that we found in Mallet and Temple. But with all his misinformation, Warton managed to get at many truths about Icelandic poetry, and his presentation of them was fresh and stimulating. Already the Old Norse mythology was well known, even down to Valhalla and the mistletoe. Old Norse poetry was well enough known to call forth this remark:

"They (the 'Runic' odes) have a certain sublime and figurative cast of diction, which is indeed one of their predominant characteristics.... When obvious terms and phrases evidently occurred, the Runic poets are fond of departing from the common and established diction. They appear to use circumlocution and comparisons not as a matter of necessity, but of choice and skill: nor are these metaphorical colourings so much the result of want of words, as of warmth of fancy." The note gives these examples: "Thus, a rainbow is called, the bridge of the gods. Poetry, the mead of Odin. The earth, the vessel that floats on ages. A ship, the horse of the waves. A tongue, the sword of words. Night, the veil of cares."

A study of the notes to Warton's dissertation reveals the fact that he had made use of the books already mentioned in the list on a previous page, and of no others that are significant. But such excellent use was made of them, that it would seem as if nothing was left in them that could be made valuable for spreading a knowledge of and an enthusiasm for Icelandic literature. When it is remembered that Warton's purpose was to prove the Saracenic origin of romantic fiction in Europe, through the Moors in Spain, and that Icelandic literature was mentioned only to account for a certain un-Arabian tinge in that romantic fiction, the wonder grows that so full and fresh a presentation of Old Norse poetry should have been made. He puts such passages as these into his illustrative notes: "Tell my mother Suanhita in Denmark, that she will not this summer comb the hair of her son. I had promised her to return, but now my side shall feel the edge of the sword." There is an appreciation of the poetic here, that makes us feel that Warton was not an unworthy wearer of the laurel. He insists that the Saxon poetry was powerfully affected by "the old scaldic fables and heroes," and gives in the text a translation of the "Battle of Brunenburgh" to prove his case. He admires "the scaldic dialogue at the tomb of Angantyr," but wrongly attributes a beautiful translation of it to Gray. He quotes at length from "a noble ode, called in the northern chronicles the Elogium of Hacon, by the scald Eyvynd; who, for his superior skill in poetry was called the Cross of Poets (Eyvindr Skalldaspillir), and fought in the battle which he celebrated."

He knows how Iceland touched England, as this passage will show: "That the Icelandic bards were common in England during the Danish invasions, there are numerous proofs. Egill, a celebrated Icelandic poet, having murthered the son and many of the friends of Eric Blodaxe, king of Denmark or Norway, then residing in Northumberland, and which he had just conquered, procured a pardon by singing before the king, at the command of his queen Gunhilde, an extemporaneous ode. Egill compliments the king, who probably was his patron, with the appellation of the English chief. 'I offer my freight to the king. I owe a poem for my ransom. I present to the ENGLISH CHIEF the mead of Odin.' Afterwards he calls this Danish conqueror the commander of the Scottish fleet. 'The commander of the Scottish fleet fattened the ravenous birds. The sister of Nera (Death) trampled on the foe: she trampled on the evening food of the eagle.'"

So wide a knowledge and so keen an appreciation of Old Norse in a Warton, whose interest was chiefly elsewhere, argues for a spreading popularity of the ancient literature. Thus far, only Gray has made living English literature out of these old stories, and he only two short poems. There were other attempts to achieve poetic success with this foreign material, but a hundred exacting years have covered them with oblivion.

DRAKE (1766-1836). MATHIAS (1754-1835).

In the second decade of the nineteenth century, Nathan Drake, M.D., made a strong effort to popularize Norse mythology and literature. The fourth edition of his work entitled *Literary Hours* (London, 1820) contains[11] an appreciative article on the subject, the fullness of which is indicated in these words from p. 309:

"The most striking and characteristic parts of the Scandinavian mythology, together with no inconsiderable portion of the manners and customs of our northern ancestors, have now passed before the reader; their theology, warfare, and poetry, their gallantry, religious rites, and superstitions, have been separately, and, I trust, distinctly reviewed."

The essay is written in an easy style that doubtless gained for it many readers. All the available knowledge of the subject was used, and a clearer view of it was presented than had been obtainable in Percy's "Mallet." The author was a thoughtful man, able to detect errors in Warton and Percy, but his zeal in his enterprise led him to praise versifiers inordinately that had used the "Gothic fables." He quotes liberally from writers whose books are not to be had in this country, and certainly the uninspired verses merit the neglect that this fact indicates. He calls Sayers' pen "masterly" that wrote these lines:

> Coucher of the ponderous spear,
> Thou shout'st amid the battle's stound--
> The armed Sisters hear,
> Viewless hurrying o'er the ground
> They strike the destin'd chiefs and call them to the skies.

(P. 168.)

From Penrose he quotes such lines as these:

> The feast begins, the skull goes round,
> Laughter shouts--the shouts resound.
> The gust of war subsides--E'en now
> The grim chief curls his cheek, and smooths his rugged brow.

(P. 171.)

From Sterling comes this imitation of Gray:

> Now the rage of combat burns,
> Haughty chiefs on chiefs lie slain;
> The battle glows and sinks by turns,
> Death and carnage load the plain.

(P 172.)

From these extracts, it appears that the poets who imitated Gray considered that only "dreadful songs," like his, were to be found in

Scandinavian poetry.

Downman, Herbert and Mathias are also adduced by Dr. Drake as examples of poets who have gained much by Old Norse borrowings, but these borrowings are invariably scenes from a chamber of horrors. It occurs to me that perhaps Dr. Drake had begun to tire of the spiritless echoes of the classical schools, and that he fondly hoped that such shrieks and groans as those he admired in this essay would satisfy his cravings for better things in poetry. But the critic had no adequate knowledge of the way in which genius works. His one desire in these studies of Scandinavian mythology was "to recommend it to the votaries of the Muse, as a machinery admirably constructed for their purpose" (p. 158). He hopes for "a more extensive adoption of the Scandinavian mythology, especially in our *epic* and *lyric* compositions" (p. 311). We smile at the notion, to-day, but that very conception of poetry as "machinery" is characteristic of a whole century of our English literature.

The Mathias mentioned by Drake is Thomas James Mathias, whose book, *Odes Chiefly from the Norse Tongue* (London, 1781), received the distinction of an American reprint (New York, 1806). Bartholinus furnishes the material and Gray the spirit for these pieces.

AMOS S. COTTLE(1768-1800). WILLIAM HERBERT (1778-1847).

In this period belong two works of translation that mark the approach of the time when Old Norse prose and poetry were to be read in the original. As literature they are of little value, and they had but slight influence on succeeding writers.

At Bristol, in 1797, was published *Icelandic Poetry, or, The Edda of*

Saemund translated into English Verse, by A.S. Cottle of Magdalen College, Cambridge. This work has an Introduction containing nothing worth discussing here, and an "Epistle" to A.S. Cottle from Robert Southey. The laureate, in good blank verse, discourses on the Old Norse heroes whom he happens to know about. They are the old favorites, Regner Lodbrog and his sons; in Southey's poem the foeman's skull is, as usual, the drinking cup. It was certainly time for new actors and new properties to appear in English versions of Scandinavian stories.

The translations are twelve in number, and evince an intelligent and facile versifier. When all is said, these old songs could contribute to the pleasure of very few. Only a student of history, or a poet, or an antiquarian, would dwell with loving interest on the lays of Vafthrudnis, Grimner, Skirner and Hymer (as Cottle spells them). Besides, they are difficult to read, and must be abundantly annotated to make them comprehensible. In such works as this of Cottle, a Scott might find wherewith to lend color to a story or a poem, but the common man would borrow Walpole's words, used in characterizing Gray's "Odes": "They are not interesting, and do not ... touch any passion; our human feelings ... are not here affected. Who can care through what horrors a Runic savage arrived at all the joys and glories they could conceive--the supreme felicity of boozing ale out of the skull of an enemy in Odin's hall?"[12]

In 1804 a book was published bearing this title-page: ***Select Icelandic Poetry, translated from the originals: with notes***. The preface was signed by the author, William Herbert. The pieces are from Saemund, Bartholinus, Verelius, and Perinskjoeld's edition of ***Heimskringla***, and were all translated with the assistance of the Latin versions. The notes are explanatory of the allusions and the hiatuses in the poems. Reference is made to MSS. of the Norse pieces existing in museums and libraries, which the author had consulted. Thus we see scholarship beginning to extend investigations. As for the verses themselves not much need be said. They are not so good as Cottle's, although they received a notice from Scott in the ***Edinburgh Review***. The thing to notice about the work is that it pretends to come direct from Old Norse, not, as most of the work dealt with so far, ***via*** Latin.

Icelandic poetry is more difficult to read than Icelandic prose, and so it seems strange that the former should have been attacked first by English scholars. Yet so it was, and until 1844 our English literature had no other inspiration in old Norse writings than the rude and rugged songs that first lent their lilt to Gray. The ***human*** North is in the sagas, and when they were revealed to our people, Icelandic literature began to mean something more than Valhalla and the mead-bouts there. The scene was changed to earth, and the gods gave place to nobler actors, men and women. The action was lifted to the eminence of a world-drama. But before the change came Sir Walter Scott, and it is fitting that the first period of Norse influence in English literature should close, as it began, with a great master.

SIR WALTER SCOTT (1771-1832).

In 1792, Walter Scott was twenty-one years old, and one of his note-books of that year contains this entry: "Vegtam's Kvitha or The Descent of Odin, with the Latin of Thomas Bartholine, and the English poetical version of Mr. Gray; with some account of the Death of Balder, both as related in the Edda, and as handed down to us by the Northern historians--***Auctore Gualtero Scott***." According to Lockhart,[13] the Icelandic, Latin and English versions were here transcribed, and the historical account that followed--seven closely written quarto pages--was read before a debating society.

It was to be expected that one so enthusiastic about antiquities as

Scott would early discover the treasury of Norse history and song. At twenty-one, as we see, he is transcribing a song in a language he knew nothing about, as well as in translations. Fourteen years later, he has learned enough about the subject to write a review of Herbert's ***Poems and Translations***.[14]

In 1813, he writes an account of the ***Eyrbyggja Saga*** for ***Illustrations of Northern Antiquities*** (edited by Robert Jameson, Edinburgh, 1814).

There are two of Scott's contributions to literature that possess more than a mere tinge of Old Norse knowledge, namely, the long poem "Harold, the Dauntless" (published in 1817), and the long story "The Pirate" (published in 1821). The poem is weak, but it illustrates Scott's theory of the usefulness of poetical antiquities to the modern poet. In another connection Scott said: "In the rude song of the Scald, we regard less the strained imagery and extravagance of epithet, than the wild impressions which it conveys of the dauntless resolution, savage superstition, rude festivity and ceaseless depredations of the ancient Scandinavians."[15] The poet did his work in accordance with this theory, and so in "Harold, the Dauntless," we note no flavor of the older poetry in phrase or in method. Harold is fierce enough and grim enough to measure up to the old ideal of a Norse hero.

"I was rocked in a buckler and fed from a blade," is his boast before his newly christened father, and in his apostrophe to his grandsire Eric, the popular notion of early Norse antiquarianism is again exhibited:

> In wild Valhalla hast thou quaffed
> From foeman's skull metheglin draught?

Scott's scholarship in Old Norse was largely derived from the Latin tomes, and such conceptions as those quoted are therefore common in his poem. That the poet realized the inadequacy of such knowledge, the review of Herbert's poetry, published in the **Edinburgh Review** for October, 1806, shows. In this article he has a vision of what shall be when men shall be able "to trace the Runic rhyme" itself.

"The Pirate," exhibited the Wizard's skill in weaving the old and the new together, the old being the traditions of the Shetlands, full of the ancestral beliefs in Old Norse things, the new being the life in those islands in a recent century. This is a stirring story, that comes into our consideration because of its Scandinavian antiquities. Again we find the Latin treasuries of Bartholinus, Torfaeus, Perinskjoeld and Olaus Magnus in evidence, though here, too, mention is made of "Haco," and Tryggvason and "Harfager." With a background of island scenery, with which Scott became familiar during a light-house inspector's voyage made in 1814, this story is a picture full of vivid colors and characters. In Norna of the Fitful Head, he has created a mysterious personage in whose mouth "Runic rhymes" are the only proper speech. She stills the tempest with them, and "The Song of the Tempest" is a strong apostrophe, though it is neither Runic nor rhymed. She preludes her life-story with verses that are rhymed but not Runic, and she sings incantations in the same wise. This **Reimkennar** is an echo of the **Voeluspa**, and is the only kind of Norse woman that the time of Scott could imagine. Claud Halcro, the poet, is fond of rhyming the only kind of Norseman known to his time, and in his "Song of Harold Harfager" we hear the echoes of Gray's odes. Scott's reading was wide in all ancient lore, and he never missed a chance to introduce an odd custom if it would make an interesting scene in his story. So here we have the "Sword Dance" (celebrated by Olaus Magnus, though I have never read of it in Old Norse), the "Questioning of the Sibyl" (like that in Gray's "Descent of Odin"), the "Capture and Sharing of the Whale," and the "Promise of Odin." In most of the natives there are turns of speech that recall the Norse ancestry of the Shetlanders.

In Scott, then, we see the lengthening out of the influence of the antiquarians who wrote of a dead past in a dead language. The time was at hand when that past was to live again, painted in the living words of living men.

III.

FROM THE SOURCES THEMSELVES.

In the preceding section we noted the achievements of English scholarship and genius working under great disadvantages. Gray and Scott may have had a smattering of Icelandic, but Latin translations were necessary to reveal the meaning of what few Old Norse texts were available to them. This paucity of material, more than the ignorance of the language, was responsible for the slow progress in popularizing the remarkable literature of the North. Scaldic and Eddie poems comprised all that was known to English readers of that literature, and in them the superhuman rather than the human elements were predominant.

We have come now to a time when the field of our view broadens to include not only more and different material, but more and different men. The sagas were annexed to the old songs, and the body of literature to attract attention was thus increased a thousand fold. The antiquarians were supplanted by scholars who, although passionately devoted to the study of the past, were still vitally interested in the affairs of the time in which they lived. The second and greatest stage of the development of Old Norse influence in England has a mark of distinction that belongs to few literary epochs. The men who made it

lived lives that were as heroic in devotion to duty and principle as
many of those written down in the sagas themselves. I have sometimes
wondered whether it is merely accidental that English saga scholars were
so often men of high soul and strong action. Certain it is that Richard
Cleasby, and Samuel Laing, and George Webbe Dasent, and Robert Lowe are
types of men that the Icelanders would have celebrated, as having "left
a tale to tell" in their full and active lives. And no less certain is
it that Thomas Carlyle, and Matthew Arnold, and William Morris, and
Charles Kingsley, and Gerald Massey labored for a better manhood that
should rise to the stature and reflect the virtues of the heroes of the
Northland.

RICHARD CLEASBY (1797-1847).

In the forties of the nineteenth century several minds began to work,
independently of one another, in this wider field of Icelandic
literature. Richard Cleasby (1797-1847), an English merchant's son with
scholarly instincts, began the study of the sagas, but made slight
progress because of what he called an "unaccountable and most scandalous
blank," the want of a dictionary. This was in 1840, and for the next
seven years he labored to fill up that blank. The record[16] of those
years is a wonderful witness to the heroism and spirit of the scholar,
and justifies Sir George Dasent's characterization of Cleasby as "one of
the most indefatigable students that ever lived." The work thus begun
was not completed until many years afterward (it is dated 1874), and, by
untoward circumstances, very little of it is Richard Cleasby's. But
generous scholarship acknowledged its debt to the man who gave his
strength and his wealth to the work, by placing his name on the
title-page. No less shall we fail to honor his memory by mentioning his
labors here. Although the dictionary was not completed in the decade of
its inception, the study that it was designed to promote took hold on a
number of men and the results were remarkable for both literature and
scholarship.

THOMAS CARLYLE (1795-1881).

First in order of time was the work of Thomas Carlyle. It will not seem strange to the student of English literature to find that this writer came under the influence of the old skalds and sagaman and spoke appreciative words concerning them. His German studies had to take cognizance of the Old Norse treasuries of poetry, and he became a diligent reader of Icelandic literature in what translations he could get at, German and English. The strongest utterance on the subject that he left behind him is in "Lecture I" of the series "On Heroes, Hero-Worship, and the Heroic in History," dated May, 1840. This is a treatment of Scandinavian mythology, rugged and thorough, like all of this man's work. Carlyle evinces a scholar's instinct in more than one place, as, for instance, when he doubts the ***grandmother*** etymology of ***Edda***, an etymology repeated until a much later day by scholars of a less sure sense.[17] But this lecture "On Heroes" is also a glorification of the literature with which we are dealing, and in this regard it is worthy of special note here.

In the first place, Carlyle with true critical instinct caught the essence of it; to him it seemed to have "a rude childlike way of recognizing the divineness of Nature, the divineness of Man." For him Scandinavian mythology was superior in sincerity to the Grecian, though it lacked the grace of the latter. "Sincerity, I think, is better than grace. I feel that these old Northmen were looking into Nature with open eye and soul: most earnest, honest; childlike, and yet manlike; with a great-hearted simplicity and depth and freshness, in a true, loving, admiring, unfearing way. A right valiant, true old race of men." This is a truer appreciation than Gray and Walpole had, eighty years before. In the second place, Carlyle was not misled into thinking that valor in war was the only characteristic of the rude Norseman, and skill in drinking his only household virtue. "Beautiful traits of pity, too, and honest pity." Then he tells of Baldur and Nanna, in his rugged prose account anticipating Matthew Arnold. Other qualities of the literature appeal to him. "I like much their robust simplicity; their veracity, directness of conception. Thor 'draws down his brows' in a veritable Norse rage; 'grasps his hammer till the **knuckles grow white**." Again; "A great broad Brobdignag grin of true humor is this Skrymir; mirth resting on earnestness and sadness, as the rainbow on the black tempest: only a right valiant heart is capable of that." Still again: "This law of mutation, which also is a law written in man's inmost thought, has been deciphered by these old earnest Thinkers in their rude style."

Thomas Carlyle, seeking to explain the worship of a pagan divinity, chose Odin as the noblest example of such a hero. The picture of Odin he drew from the prose Edda, mainly, and his purpose required that he paint the picture in the most attractive colors. So it happened that our English literature got its first **complete** view of Old Norse ethics and art. The memory of Gray's "dreadful songs" had ruled for almost a century, and ordinary readers might be pardoned for thinking that Old Norse literature, like Old Norse history, was written in blood. We have seen that Gray's imitators perpetuated the old idea, and that even Scott sanctioned it, and now we see England's emancipation from it. The grouty old Scotchman of Craigenputtoch knew no more Icelandic than most of his fellow countrymen (be it noted that he said: "From the Humber upwards, all over Scotland, the speech of the common people is still in a singular degree Icelandic, its Germanism has still a peculiar Norse tinge"); but he saw far more deeply into the heart of Icelandic literature than anybody before him. His emphasis of its many sidedness, of its sincerity, its humanity, its simplicity, its directness, its humor and its wisdom, was the signal for a change in the popular estimation of its worth to our modern art. Since his day we have had Morris and Arnold and a host of minor singers, and the nineteenth century revival of interest in Old Norse literature.

The other work by Carlyle dealing directly with Old Norse material is *The Early Kings of Norway*. Here he digests *Heimskringla*, which was obtainable through Laing's translation, in a way to stir the blood. The story, as he tells it, is breathlessly interesting, and it is a pity that readers of Carlyle so often stop short of this work. As in the *Hero-Worship*, he shows this Teutonic bias, and the religious training that minified Greek literature.

Snorri's work elicits from him repeated applause. Here, for instance, in Chap. X: "It has, all of it, the description (and we see clearly the fact itself had), a kind of pathetic grandeur, simplicity, and rude nobleness; something Epic or Homeric, without the metre or the singing of Homer, but with all the sincerity, rugged truth to nature, and much more of piety, devoutness, reverence for what is ever high in this universe, than meets us in those old Greek Ballad-mongers."

SAMUEL LAING (1780-1868).

It was the work of Samuel Laing that gave Carlyle the material for this last-mentioned book.[18] Laing's translation of *Heimskringla* bears the date 1844, and although Mr. Dasent's quaint version of the *Prose Edda* preceded it by two years, *The Sagas of the Norse Kings* was the "epoch-making" book. It is true that a later version has superseded it in literary and scholarly finish, but Laing's work was a pioneer of sterling intrinsic value, and many there be that do it homage still. Laing had the laudable ambition--so seldom found in these days--"to give a plain, faithful translation into English of the *Heimskringla*, unencumbered with antiquarian research, and suited to the plain English reader."[19] With this work, then, Icelandic lore passes out of the hands of the antiquarian into the hands of common readers. It matters little that the audience is even still fit and few; from this time on he that runs may read.

For our purpose it will not be necessary to characterize the translation. Laing commanded an excellent style, and he was enthusiastic over his work. Indeed, the commonest criticism passed on the "Preliminary Dissertation" was that the author's zeal had run away with his good sense. Be that as it may, Laing called the attention of his readers to the neglect of a literature and a history which should be England's pride, as Anglo-Saxon literature and history even then were. The reviews of the time made it appear as if another Battle of the Books were impending--Anglo-Saxon versus Icelandic; a writer in the ***English Review*** (Vol. 82, p. 316), pro-Saxon in his zeal, admitting at last that "of none of the children of the Norse, whether Goth or Frank, Saxon or Scandinavian, have the others any reason to be ashamed. All have earned the gratitude and admiration of the world, and their combined or successive efforts have made England and Europe what they are."

It is refreshing to come upon new views of Old Norse character, that recognize "amidst anarchy and bloodshed, redeeming features of kindliness and better feeling which tell of the mingled principles that war within our nature for the mastery." Laing's translation accomplished this for English readers, and with the years came a deeper knowledge that showed those touches of tenderness and traits of beauty which, even in 1844, were not perceptible to those readers.

HENRY WADSWORTH LONGFELLOW (1807-1882).

JAMES RUSSELL LOWELL (1819-1891).

The Story of the Norse Kings, thus translated by an Englishman, suggested to our American poet, Longfellow, a series of lyrics on King

Olaf. The young college professor that wrote about *Frithjof's Saga* in the ***North American Review*** for 1837, was bound, sooner or later, to come back to the field when he found that the American reading public would listen to whatever songs he sang to them. Before 1850, Longfellow had written "The Challenge of Thor," a poem which imitated the form of Icelandic verse and catches much of its spirit. In 1859, the thought came to him "that a very good poem might be written on the Saga of King Olaf, who converted the North to Christianity." Two years later he completed the lyrics that compose "The Musician's Tale" in ***The Tales of a Wayside Inn***, published in 1863, and in this work "The Challenge of Thor" serves as a prelude. The pieces after this prelude are not imitations of the Icelandic verse, but are like Tegner's *Frithjof's Saga*, in that each new portion has a meter of its own. There is not, either, a consistent effort to put the flavor of the North into the poetry, so that, properly speaking, we have here only the retelling of an old tale. The ballad fervor and movement are often perceptible, though nowhere does the poet strike the ringing note of "The Skeleton in Armor," published in the volume of 1841.

Truth to tell, Longfellow's "Saga of King Olaf" is not a remarkable work. One who reads the few chapters in Carlyle's ***Early Kings of Norway*** that deal with Olaf Tryggvason gets more of the fire and spirit of the old saga at every turning. The poet chooses scenes and incidents very skilfully, but for their proper presentation a terseness is necessary that is not reconcilable with frequent rhymes. Compare the saga account with the poem's: "What is this that has broken?" asked King Olaf. "Norway from thy hand, King," answered Tamberskelver.

> "What was that?" said Olaf, standing
> On the quarter deck.
> "Something heard I like the stranding
> Of a shattered wreck."
> Einar then, the arrow taking

From the loosened string,
Answered, "That was Norway breaking
From thy hand, O King!"

Nevertheless, Longfellow is to be thanked for acquainting a wide circle of readers with the sterling saga literature.

One other American poet was busy with the ancient Northern literature at this time. James Russell Lowell wrote one notable poem that is Old Norse in subject and spirit, "The Voyage to Vinland." The third part of the poem, "Gudrida's Prophecy," hints at Icelandic versification, and the short lines are hammer-strokes that warm the reader to enthusiasm. Far more of the spirit of the old literature is in this short poem than is to be found in the whole of Longfellow's "Saga of King Olaf." The character of Bioern is well drawn, recalling Bodli, of Morris' poem, in its principal features. Certainly there is a reflection here of that Old Norse conception of life which gave to men's deeds their due reward, and which exalted the power of will. This poem was begun in 1850, but was not published till 1868.

In Lowell's poems are to be found many figures and allusions pointing to his familiarity with Icelandic song and story. At the end of the third strophe of the "Commemoration Ode," for instance, Truth is pictured as Brynhild,

plumed and mailed,
With sweet, stern face unveiled.

In these borrowings of themes and allusions, Lowell is at one with most of the poets of the present day. It used to be the fashion, and is still, for tables of contents in volumes of verse to show titles like these: "Prometheus"; "Iliad VIII, 542-561"; "Alectryon." Present-day volumes are becoming more and more besprinkled with titles like these:

"Balder the Beautiful"; "The Death of Arnkel," etc. In this fact alone is seen the turn of the tide. Heroes and heroines in dramas and novels are beginning to bear Old Norse names, even where the setting is not northern; witness Sidney Dobell's **Balder**, where not even a single allusion is made to Icelandic matters.

MATTHEW ARNOLD (1822-1888).

Matthew Arnold's strong sympathy with noble and virile literature of whatever age or nation led him in time to Old Norse, and his poem "Balder Dead" is of distinct importance among the works of the nineteenth century in English literature. It is an addition of permanent value to our poetry, because of its marked originality and its high ethical tone. "Mallet, and his version of the Edda, is all the poem is based upon," says Arnold.[20] It is the poet's divinely implanted instinct that gathers from the few chapters of an old book a knowledge wonderfully full and deep of the cosmogony and eschatology of the northern nations of Europe. "Balder Dead" tells the familiar story of the whitest of the gods, but it also contains the essence of Old Icelandic religion; indeed there is no single short work in our language which gives a tithe of the information about the North, its spirit, and its philosophy, which this poem of Matthew Arnold's sets forth. In future days a text-book of original English poems will be in the hands of our boys and girls which will enable them to get, through the medium of their own language, the message and the spirit of foreign literature. Old Norse song will need no other representative than Matthew Arnold's "Balder Dead."

This is an original poem. It does not imitate the verse nor the word of the older song, but the flavor of it is here. Gray and his imitators drew from the Icelandic fountain "dreadful songs" and many poets since have heard no milder note. Matthew Arnold's instincts were for peace and the arts of peace, and he found in Balder a type for the ennobling of our own century. Balder says to his brother who has come to lament that Lok's machinations will keep the best beloved of the gods in Niflheim:

> For I am long since weary of your storm
> Of carnage, and find, Hermod, in your life
> Something too much of war and broils, which make
> Life one perpetual fight, a bath of blood.
> Mine eyes are dizzy with the arrowy hail;
> Mine ears are stunn'd with blows, and sick for calm.

Arnold has exalted the Revelator of the Northern mythology, and in magnificent poetry sets forth his apocalyptic vision:

> Unarm'd, inglorious; I attend the course
> Of ages, and my late return to light,
> In times less alien to a spirit mild,
> In new-recover'd seats, the happier day.

> .   .   .   .

> Far to the south, beyond the blue, there spreads
> Another Heaven, the boundless--no one yet
> Hath reach'd it; there hereafter shall arise
> The second Asgard, with another name.

> .   .   .   .

> There re-assembling we shall see emerge
> From the bright Ocean at our feet an earth
> More fresh, more verdant than the last, with fruits
> Self-springing, and a seed of man preserved,
> Who then shall live in peace, as now in war.

Here is the grandest message that the Old Norse religion had to give, and Matthew Arnold concerned himself with that alone. It is a far cry from Regner Lodbrog to this. There is a fine touch in the introduction of Regner into the lamentation of Balder. Arnold makes the old warrior say of the ruder skalds:

> But they harp ever on one string, and wake
> Remembrance in our souls of war alone,
> Such as on earth we valiantly have waged,
> And blood, and ringing blows, and violent death.
> But when thou sangest, Balder, thou didst strike
> Another note, and, like a bird in spring,
> Thy voice of joyance minded us, and youth,
> And wife, and children, and our ancient home.

Here is a human Norseman, a figure not often presented in the versions of the old stories that English poets and romancers have given us. Arnold did a good service to Icelandic literature when he put into Regner's mouth mild sentiments and a love for home and family. The note is not lacking in the ancient literature, but it took Englishmen three centuries to find it. It was the scholar, Matthew Arnold, who first repeated the gentler strain in the rude music of the North, as it was the scholar, Thomas Gray, who first echoed the "dreadful songs" of that old psalmody. Gray has all the culture of his age, when it was still possible to compass all knowledge in one lifetime; Arnold had all the literary culture of his fuller century when multiplied sciences force a scholar to be content with one segment of human knowledge. The former had music and architecture and other sciences among his accomplishments; the latter spread out in literature, as "Sohrab and Rustum," "Empedocles on Etna," "Tristram and Iseult," as well as "Balder Dead" attest. The quatrain prefixed to the volume containing the narrative and elegiac poems be-tokens what joy Arnold had in his literary work, and indicates why these poems cannot fail to live:

What poets feel not, when they make,
A pleasure in creating,
The world in its turn will not take
Pleasure in contemplating.

Balder is the creation of Old Norse poetry that is most popular with contemporary English writers, and Matthew Arnold first made him so. As Bugge points out, no deed of his is "celebrated in song or story. His personality only is described; of his activity in life almost no external trait is recorded. All the stress is laid upon his death; and, like Christ, Baldr dies in his youth."[21]

SIR GEORGE WEBBE DASENT (1820-1896).

Among the scholars who have labored to give England the benefit of a fuller and truer knowledge of Norse matters, none will be remembered more gratefully than Sir George Webbe Dasent. Known to the reading public most widely by his translations of the folk-tales of Asbjoernsen and Moe, he has still a claim upon the attention of the students of Icelandic. As we have seen, he gave out a translation of the *Younger Edda* in 1842, and during the half century and more that followed he wrote other works of history and literature connected with our subject. Two saga translations were published in 1861 and 1866, *The Story of Burnt Njal*, and *The Story of Gisli the Outlaw*, which will always rank high in this class of literature. *Njala* especially is an excellent piece of work, a classic among translations. The "Prolegomena" is rich in information, and very little of it has been superseded by later scholarship. In 1887 and 1894 he translated for the Master of the Rolls, *The Orkney Saga* and *The Saga of Hakon*, the texts of which Vigfusson had printed in the same series some years before. The interest of the government in Icelandic annals connected with English history is indicated in these last publications, and England is fortunate to have had such enthusiastic scholars as Vigfusson and Dasent to do the work. These men had been collaborators on the Cleasby Dictionary, and in this work as in all others Dasent displayed an eagerness to have his countrymen know how significant England's relationship to Iceland was. He was as certain as Laing had been before him of the preeminence of this literature among the mediaeval writings. Like Laing, too, he would have the general reader turn to this body of work "which for its beauty and richness is worthy of being known to the greatest possible number of readers."[22]

To mark the progress away from the old conception of unmitigated brutality these words of Dasent stand here:[23] "The faults of these Norsemen were the faults of their time; their virtues they possessed in larger measure than the rest of their age, and thus when Christianity had tamed their fury, they became the torch-bearers of civilization; and though the plowshare of Destiny, when it planted them in Europe, uprooted along its furrow many a pretty flower of feeling in the lands which felt the fury of these Northern conquerers, their energy and endurance gave a lasting temper to the West, and more especially to England, which will wear so long as the world wears, and at the same time implanted principles of freedom which shall never be rooted out. Such results are a compensation for many bygone sorrows."

CHARLES KINGSLEY (1819-1875).

In 1874, Charles Kingsley visited America and delivered some lectures. Among these was one entitled "The First Discovery of America." This interests us here because it displays an appreciation, if not a deep knowledge, of Icelandic literature. In it the lecturer commended to Longfellow's attention a ballad sung in the Faroes, begging him to translate it some day, "as none but he can translate it." "It is so sad, that no tenderness less exquisite than his can prevent its being painful; and at least in its **denouement**, so naive, that no purity less exquisite than his can prevent its being dreadful."[24] Later in the lecture he commends to his hearers the **Heimskringla** of Snorri Sturluson, the "Homer of the North."[25]

Speaking of the elements that mingled to produce the British character, Kingsley says: "In manners as well as in religion, the Norse were humanized and civilized by their contact with the Celts, both in Scotland and in Ireland. Both peoples had valor, intellect, imagination: but the Celt had that which the burly, angular Norse character, however deep and stately, and however humorous, wanted; namely, music of nature, tenderness, grace, rapidity, playfulness; just the qualities, combining with the Scandinavian (and in Scotland with the Angle) elements of character which have produced, in Ireland and in Scotland, two schools of lyric poetry second to none in the world."[26] Over the page, Kingsley has this to say: "For they were a sad people, those old Norse forefathers of ours."[27] Humorous and sad are not inconsistent words in these sentences; the Norseman had a sense of the ludicrous, and could jest grimly in the face of death. Of the sadness of his life, no one needs to be told who has read a saga or two. Kingsley says: "There is, in the old sagas, none of that enjoyment of life which shines out everywhere in Greek poetry, even through its deepest tragedies. Not in complacency with Nature's beauty, but in the fierce struggle with her wrath, does the Norseman feel pleasure."[28]

This lecture shows a deeper acquaintance with Old Norse literature than Kingsley was willing to acknowledge. Not only are the stories well chosen which he uses throughout, but the intuitions are sound, and the inferences based upon them. He anticipated the work of this investigation in the last words of the address. He has been telling the fine story of Thormod at Sticklestead:

"I shall not insult your intelligence by any comment or even epithet of my own. I shall but ask you, Was not this man your kinsman? Does not the story sound, allowing for all change of manners as well as of time and place, like a scene out of your own Bret Harte or Colonel John Hay's writings; a scene of the dry humor, the rough heroism of your own far West? Yes, as long as you have your *Jem Bludsos* and *Tom Flynns of Virginia City*, the old Norse blood is surely not extinct, the old Norse spirit is not dead."[29]

EDMUND GOSSE (1849-).

Among contemporary English poets who have taught the world of readers that things Norse are worthy of attention, is Edmund Gosse. He has been more intimately connected with the popularization of modern Norwegian literature, notably of Ibsen, but he has also found in Old Norse story themes for poetic treatment. We mention "The Death of Arnkel," found in the volume *Firdausi in Exile*, more because it shows that our poets are turning to *the gesta islandicorum* for themes, than because it is a remarkable poem. More pretentious is *King Erik, a Tragedy*, London, 1876. Here is a noble drama which displays an intimate acquaintance with the literature that gave it its themes and inspiration. The author dedicates it to Robert Browning, calling it:

> ... this lyric symbol of my labour,
> This antique light that led my dreams so long,
> This battered hull of a barbaric tabor,
> Beaten to runic song.

I have often thought that fate was very unkind to keep Browning so persistently in the south of Europe, when, in Iceland and Norway, were mines that he could have worked in to such supreme advantage. To be sure his method clashes with the simplicity of the Old Norse manner, but from him we should have had men and women superb in stature and virility, and perhaps the Arctic influence would have killed the troublesome tropicality of his language.

This drama by Gosse is not strictly Icelandic in motive. Jealousy was not the passion to loosen the tongue of the sagaman, and in so far as that is the theme of "King Erik," the play is not Old Norse in origin. Christian material, too, has been introduced that gives a modern tinge to the drama, but there is enough of the genuine saga spirit to warrant attention to it here. Something more than the names is Icelandic. Here is a woman, Botilda, with strength of character enough to recall a Brynhild or a Bergthora. Gisli is the foster-brother that takes up the blood-feud for Grimur. Adalbjoerg and Svanhilda are the whisperers of slander and the workers of ill. Marcus is the skald who is making a poem about the king. Here are customs and beliefs distinctly Norse:

> I loved him from the first,
> And so the second midnight to the cliff
> We went. I mind me how the round moon rose,
> And how a great whale in the offing plunged,
> Dark on the golden circle. There we cut
> A space of turf, and lifted it, and ran
> Our knife-points sharp into our arms, and drew
> Blood that dripped into the warm mould and mixed.
> So there under the turf our plighted faith
> Starts in the dew of grasses.

(Act. IV, Sc. II.)

But all day long I hear amid the crowds,

·   ·   ·   ·   ·   ·   ·   ·   ·   ·

A voice that murmurs in a monotone,
Strange, warning words that scarcely miss the ear,
Yet miss it altogether.

Botilda.

Oh! God grant,
You be not fey, nor truly near your end!

(Act. IV, Sc. III.)

Although this work is dramatic in form, it is not so in spirit. The true dramatist would have put such an incident as the swearing of brotherhood into a scene, instead of into a speech. This effort is, however, the nearest approach to a drama in English founded on saga material. It is curious that our poets have inclined to every form but the drama in reproducing Old Norse literature. It is not that saga-stuff is not dramatic in possibilities. Ewald and Oehlenschlaeger have used this material to excellent effect in Danish dramas. Had the sagas been accessible to Englishmen in Shakespeare's time, we should certainly have had dramas of Icelandic life.

IV.

BY THE HAND OF THE MASTER.

Time has brought us to the man whose work in this field needs no apology. The writer whom we consider next contributed almost as much material to the English treasury of Northern gold as did all the writers we have so far considered. Were it not for William Morris, the examination that we are making would not not be worth while. The name *literature*, in its narrow sense, belongs to only a few of the writings that we have examined up to this point, but what we are now to inspect deserves that title without the shadow of a doubt. For that reason we set in a separate chapter the examination of Morris' Old Norse adaptations and creations.

WILLIAM MORRIS (1834-1896).

The biographer of William Morris fixes 1868 as the beginning of the poet's Icelandic stories.[30] Eirikr Magnusson, an Icelander, was his guide, and the pupil made rapid progress. Dasent's work had drawn Morris' attention to the sagas, and within a few months most of the sagas had been read in the original. Although *The Saga of Gunnlang Worm-tongue* was published in the *Fortnightly Review*, for January, 1869, the *Grettis Saga*, of April, was the first published book on an Old Norse subject. The next year gave the *Voelsunga Saga*. In 1871, Morris made a journey through Iceland, the fruits of which were afterwards seen in many a noble work. In 1875, *Three Northern Love Stories* was published, and, in 1877, *The Story of Sigurd the Volsung and the Fall of the Niblungs*. More than ten years passed before he turned again to Icelandic work, the Romances of the years of 1889 to 1896 showing signs of it, and the translations in the *Saga Library*, "Howard the Halt," "The Banded Men," *Eyrbyggja* and *Heimskringla* of 1891-95. These contributions to the subject of our examination are no less valuable than voluminous, and we make no excuses for an extended consideration of them. They deserve a wider public than they have yet attained.

1.

The Story of Grettir the Strong is the title of Morris and Magnusson's version of the *Grettis Saga*. The version impresses the reader as one made with loving care by artistic hands. Certainly English readers will read no other translation of this work, for this one is satisfactory as a version and as an art-work. English readers will here get all the flavor of the original that it is possible to get in a translation, and those who can read Icelandic if put to it, will prefer to get *Grettla* through Morris and Magnusson. All the essentials are here, if not all the nuances.

The reader unfamiliar with sagas will need a little patience with the genealogies that crop out in every chapter. The sagaman has a squirrel-like agility in climbing family trees, and he is well acquainted with their interlocking branches. There are chapters in the *Grettis Saga* where this vanity runs riot, and makes us suspect that Iceland differed little from a country town of to-day in its love for gossip about the family of neighbors whose names happen to come into the conversation. If the reader will persevere through the early chapters, until Grettir commands exclusive attention, he will come to a drama which has not many peers in literature. The outlaw kills a man in every other chapter, but this record is no vulgar list of brutal fights. Not inhuman nature, but human nature is here shown, human nature struggling with unrelenting fate, making a grand fight, and coming to its end because it must, but without ignominy. How fine a touch it is that refuses to the outlaw's murderer the price set upon Grettir's head, because the getting of it was through a "nithings-deed," the murder of a dying man! William Morris was most felicitous in envoys and dedicating poems, and in the sonnet prefixed to this translation he was particularly happy. The first eight lines describe the hero of the saga--the last six lines the significance of this literary creation:

> A life scarce worth the living, a poor fame
> Scarce worth the winning, in a wretched land,
> Where fear and pain go upon either hand,
> As toward the end men fare without an aim
> Unto the dull grey dark from whence they came:
> Let them alone, the unshadowed sheer rocks stand
> Over the twilight graves of that poor band,
> Who count so little in the great world's game!
>
> Nay, with the dead I deal not; this man lives,
> And that which carried him through good and ill,
> Stern against fate while his voice echoed still
> From rock to rock, now he lies silent, strives
> With wasting time, and through its long lapse gives
> Another friend to me, life's void to fill.

2.

In the three volumes of *The Earthly Paradise*, published by William Morris in 1868-1870, there are three poems which hail from Old Norse originals. They are "The Land East of the Sun and West of the Moon," and "The Lovers of Gudrun," in Vol. II, and "The Fostering of Aslaug," in Vol. III. Of these "The Lovers of Gudrun" forms a class by itself; it is a poem to be reckoned with when the dozen greatest poems of the century are listed. The late Laureate may have equalled it in the best of the *Idylls of the King*, but he never excelled it. Let us look at it in detail.

First, be it said that "The Lovers of Gudrun" overtops all the other poems in *The Earthly Paradise*. It would be possible to prove that Morris was at his best when he worked with Old Norse material, but that task shall not detain us now. It is enough to note that the "Prologue" to *The Earthly Paradise*, called "The Wanderers," makes the leader of these wanderers, who turn story-tellers when they reach the city by "the borders of the Grecian sea," a Norseman. Born in Byzantium of a Greek mother, he claimed Norway as his home, and on his father's death returned to his kin. His speech to the Elder of the City reveals a touching loyalty to his father's home and traditions:

> But when I reached one dying autumn-tide
> My uncle's dwelling near the forest-side,
> And saw the land so scanty and so bare,
> And all the hard things men contend with there,
> A little and unworthy land it seemed,
> And yet the more of Asagard I dreamed,
> And worthier seemed the ancient faith of praise.

Here is the man, William Morris, in perfect miniature. Modern life and training had given him a speech and aspect quite suave and cultured, but the blood that flowed in his veins was red, and the tincture of iron was in it. In religion, in art, in poetry, in economics, he loved the past better than the present, though he was never unconscious of "our glorious gains." In all departments of thought the scanty, the bare, the hard, the unworthy, drew first his attention and then his love and enthusiastic praise. And so perhaps it is explained that of all the poems in *The Earthly Paradise*, the one indited first in the scarred and dreadful land where neither wheat nor wine is at home, shall be the finest in this latter-day retelling.

The first seventy years of the thirteenth century were the blossoming time of the historic saga in Iceland, and those writings that record the doings of the families of the land form, with the old songs and the best of the kingly sagas, the flower of Northern literature. These family records never extend over more than one generation, and sometimes they deal with but a few years. They are half-way between romance and history, with the balance oftenest in favor of truth. In this group are found *Egils Saga*, known at second hand to Warton, the *Eyrbyggja Saga*, translated by Walter Scott, and the *Laxdaela Saga*. It is the *Laxdaela Saga* that gives the story told by Morris in "The Lovers of Gudrun." Among sagas it is famous for its fine portrayal of character.

The saga and the poem tell the story of two neighboring farms, Herdholt and Bathsted, whose sons and daughters work out a dire tragedy. Kiartan and Bodli are the son and foster-son of the first house, and Gudrun is the daughter of the second. These are the principal personages in the drama, though the list of the other *dramatis personae* is a long one. Not only in the name of its heroine does the story suggest the *Nibelungenlied*. The machinery of the Norse stories resembles the German story's in many of its parts. In this version of Morris, the main features of the saga are kept, and distracting details are properly subordinated to the principal interest. Through the nineteen divisions of this story the interest moves rapidly, and wonder as to the issue is never lost. As a story-teller, Morris is distinctly powerful in this poem, and all the qualities that endear the story-teller to us are here found joined to many that make the poet a favorite with us. There are no lyrics in the poem--the original saga was without the song-snatches that are often found in sagas--but there are dramatic scenes that recall the power of the Master-poet. Least of all the poems in the *Earthly Paradise* does "The Lovers of Gudrun" show the Chaucerian influence, and the reader must be captious indeed who complains of the length of this story.

To the unenlightened reader this poem reveals no traits that are un-English. What there is of Old Norse flavor here is purely spiritual. The original story being in prose, no attempt could be made to keep original characteristics in verse-form. So "The Lovers of Gudrun" can stand on its own merits as an English poem; no excuses need be made for it on the plea that it is a translation.

Local color is not laid on the canvas after the figures have been painted, but all the tints in the persons and the things are grandly Norse. This story is a true romance, in that the scene is far removed from the present day, and the atmosphere is very different from our own. This story is a true picture of life, in that it sets forth the doings of men and women in the power of the master passion. And so for the purposes of literature this poem is not Norse, or rather, it is more than Norse, it is universal. Now and then, to be sure, the displaced Norse ideals are set forth in the poem, but in such wise that we almost regret that the old order has passed away. The Wanderer who tells the tale assures his listeners of the truth of it in these last words of the interlude between "The Story of Rhodope" and "The Lovers of Gudrun":

> Know withal that we
> Have ever deemed this tale as true to be,
> As though those very Dwellers in Laxdale,
> Risen from the dead had told us their own tale;
> Who for the rest while yet they dwelt on earth
> Wearied no God with prayers for more of mirth
> Than dying men have; nor were ill-content

Because no God beside their sorrow went
Turning to flowery sward the rock-strewn way,
Weakness to strength, or darkness into day.
Therefore, no marvels hath my tale to tell,
But deals with such things as men know too well;
All that I have herein your hearts to move,
Is but the seed and fruit of bitter love.

It is aside from our purpose to tell this story here. The more we study this marvelous work, the more it is impressed upon us that in the reign of love all men and all literatures are one. To the Englishman this description of an Iceland maiden is no stranger than it was to the men who sat about the spluttering fire in the Icelander's hall. It is the form of Gudrun that is here described:

That spring was she just come to her full height,
Low-bosomed yet she was, and slim and light,
Yet scarce might she grow fairer from that day;
Gold were the locks wherewith the wind did play,
Finer than silk, waved softly like the sea
After a three days' calm, and to her knee
Wellnigh they reached; fair were the white hands laid
Upon the door posts where the dragons played;
Her brow was smooth now, and a smile began
To cross her delicate mouth, the snare of man.

(*Earthly Paradise*, Vol. II, p. 247.)

Not less accustomed are we to such heroes as Kiartan:

And now in every mouth was Kiartan's name,
And daily now must Gudrun's dull ears bear
Tales of the prowess of his youth to hear,

While in his cairn forgotten lay her love.
For this man, said they, all men's hearts did move,
Nor yet might envy cling to such an one,
So far beyond all dwellers 'neath the sun;
Great was he, yet so fair of face and limb
That all folk wondered much, beholding him,
How such a man could be; no fear he knew,
And all in manly deeds he could outdo;
Fleet-foot, a swimmer strong, an archer good,
Keen-eyed to know the dark waves' changing mood;
Sure on the crag, and with the sword so skilled,
That when he played therewith the air seemed filled
With light of gleaming blades; therewith was he
Of noble speech, though says not certainly
My tale, that aught of his he left behind
With rhyme and measure deftly intertwined.

(P. 266.)

The Old Norse touch here is in the last three lines which intimate that the warrior was often a bard; but be it remembered that the Elizabethan warrior could turn a sonnet, too.

We have said that the **Laxdaela Saga** is famous for its portrayal of character. This English version falls not at all below the original in this quality. The lines already quoted show Gudrun and Kiartan as to exterior. But this is a drama of flesh and blood creations, and they are men and women that move through it, not puppets. Souls are laid bare here, in quivering, pulsating agony. The tremendous figure of this story is not Kiartan, nor Gudrun, nor Refna, but Bodli, and certainly English narrative poetry has no second creation like to him. The mind reverts to Shakespeare to find fit companionship for Bodli in poetry, and to George Eliot and Thomas Hardy in prose. The suggestion of Shakespearean qualities in George Eliot has been made by several great critics, among them Edmond Scherer;[31] in Hardy and Morris, here, we find the same soul-searching powers. These writers have created sufferers of titanic greatness, and in the presence of their tragedies we are dumb.

An English artist has made Napoleon's voyage on H.M.S. ***Bellerophon*** to his prison-isle a picture that the memory refuses to forget. The picture of Bodli as he sails back to Iceland, which, though his home, is to be his prison and his death, is no less impressive:

> Fair goes the ship that beareth out Christ's truth
> Mingled of hope, of sorrow, and of ruth,
> And on the prow Bodli the Christian stands,
> Sunk deep in thought of all the many lands
> The world holds, and the folk that dwell therein,
> And wondering why that grief and rage and sin
> Was ever wrought; but wondering most of all
> Why such wild passion on his heart should fall.

(P. 294.)

Here we have the poet's conception--and the sagaman's--of Bodli--a man in the grip of terrible Fate, who can no more swerve from the paths she marks out for him than he can add a cubit to his stature. The Greek tragedy embodies this idea, and Old Norse literature is full of it. Thomas Hardy gives it later in his contemporary novels. We sympathize with Bodli's fate because his agony is so terrible, and we call him the most striking figure in this story. But the others suffer, too, Gudrun, Kiartan, Refna; they make a stand against their woe, and utter brave words in the face of it. Only Bodli floats downward with the tide, unresisting. Guest prophesies bitter things for Gudrun, but adds:

> Be merry yet! these things shall not be all

That unto thee in this thy life shall fall.

(P. 254.)

And Gudrun takes heart. When Thurid tells her brother Kiartan that Gudrun has married another, his joy is shivered into atoms before him. But he can say, even then:

> Now is this world clean changed for me
> In this last minute, yet indeed I see
> That still it will go on for all my pain;
> Come then, my sister, let us back again;
> I must meet folk, and face the life beyond,
> And, as I may, walk 'neath the dreadful bond
> Of ugly pain--such men our fathers were,
> Not lightly bowed by any weight of care.

(P. 311.)

And Kiartan does his work in the world. Poor Refna, when she has married Kiartan hears women talking of the love that still is between Gudrun and Kiartan. She goes to Kiartan with the story, beginning with words whose pathos must conquer the most stoical of readers:

> Indeed of all thy grief I knew,
> But deemed if still thou saw'st me kind and true,
> Not asking too much, yet not failing aught
> To show that not far off need love be sought,
> If thou shouldst need love--if thou sawest all this,
> Thou wouldst not grudge to show me what a bliss
> Thy whole love was, by giving unto me
> As unto one who loved thee silently,
> Now and again the broken crumbs thereof:

Alas! I, having then no part in love,
Knew not how naught, naught can allay the soul
Of that sad thirst, but love untouched and whole!
Kinder than e'er I durst have hoped thou art,
Forgive me then, that yet my craving heart
Is so unsatisfied; I know that thou
Art fain to dream that I am happy now,
And for that seeming ever do I strive;
Thy half-love, dearest, keeps me still alive
To love thee; and I bless it--but at whiles,--

(P. 343)

And thus she gains strength to live her life.

Here, then, in Bodli, is another of the great tragic figures in
literature--a sick man. There are many of them, even in the highest rank
of literary creations, Hamlet, Lear, Othello, Macbeth! Wrong-headed,
defective as they are, we would not have them otherwise. The pearl of
greatest price is the result of an abnormal or morbid process.

Bodli comes to us from Icelandic literature, and in that fact we note
the solidarity of poetic geniuses. Not only is the great figure of Bodli
proof of this solidarity, but many other features of this poem prove it.
"Lively feeling for a situation and power to express it constitute the
poet," said Goethe. There are dramatic situations in "The Lovers of
Gudrun" which hold the reader in a breathless state till the last word
is said, and then leave him marveling at the imagination that could
conceive the scene, and the power that could express it. There are
gentler scenes, too, in the poem, where beauty and grace are conceived
as fair as ever poet dreamed, and the workmanship is thoroughly
adequate. As an example of the first, take the scene of Bodli's mourning
over Kiartan's dead body. It is here that we get that knowledge of

Bodli's woe that robs us of a cause against him. What agony is that which can speak thus over the body of the dead rival!

> ... Didst thou quite
> Know all the value of that dear delight
> As I did? Kiartan, she is changed to thee;
> Yea, and since hope is dead changed too to me,
> What shall we do, if, each of each forgiven,
> We three shall meet at last in that fair heaven
> The new faith tells of? Thee and God I pray
> Impute it not for sin to me to-day,
> If no thought I can shape thereof but this:
> O friend, O friend, when thee I meet in bliss,
> Wilt thou not give my love Gudrun to me,
> Since now indeed thine eyes made clear can see
> That I of all the world must love her most?

(P. 368.)

Examples of the gentler scenes are scattered lavishly throughout the poem and it is not necessary to enumerate.

One other sign that the Icelandic sagaman's art was kin to the English poet's. The last line of this poem is given thus by Morris:

> I did the worst to him I loved the most.

These are the very words of Gudrun in the saga, and summing up as they do her opinion of Kiartan, they stand as a model of that compression which is so admired in our poetry. Many such **multum in parvo** lines are found in Morris' poem, and at times they have a beauty that is marvelous. Joined with this quality is the special merit of Morris--picturesqueness, and so the reader often feels, when he has finished a book by Morris, like the Cook tourist after he has "done" a country of Europe--it must be done again and again to give it its due.

Of the other two Old Norse poems in **The Earthly Paradise** not much need be said. "The Land East of the Sun and West of the Moon" is a fairy tale, in the strain of Morris' prose romances. It was suggested by Thorpe's **Yule-tide Stories**, the tale coming from the **Voelundar Saga**. There is a witchery about it that makes it pleasant reading in a dreamy hour, but except the names and a few scenes about the farmstead, there is nothing Icelandic about it. The virile element of the best Icelandic literature is wanting here, and the hero's excuse for leaving weapons at home when he goes to his watch is not at all natural:

> Withal I shall not see
> Men-folk belike, but faerie,
> And all the arms within the seas
> Should help me naught to deal with these;
> Rather of such love were I fain
> As fell to Sigurd Fafnir's-bane
> When of the dragon's heart he ate.

(Vol. II, p. 33.)

This passage is nominally in the same meter as the opening lines of the poem:

> In this your land there once did dwell
> A certain carle who lived full well,
> And lacked few things to make him glad;
> And three fair sons this goodman had.

According to old time English prosody, it is the same, too, as the meter of Scott's Marmion!

In the passages quoted from "The Lovers of Gudrun" we see a measure called the same as that of Pope's *Essay on Man*! Not seldom in "The Lovers" do we forget that the lines are rhymed in twos; indeed, often we do not note the rhyme at all. We are sometimes tempted to think that in this piece, if not in "The Land East of the Sun," rhyme might have been dispensed with altogether, since it often forces archaic words and expressions into use. But it is to be said generally of Morris's management of the meter in the Old Norse pieces, that it was adequate to gain his end always, whether that end was to tell an Old Norse story in English, or to carry over an Old Norse spirit into English. Of this second achievement we shall speak further in considering *Sigurd the Volsung*.

There is one more tale in *The Earthly Paradise* which originated in Norse legend. "The Fostering of Aslaug" is drawn from Thorpe's *Northern Mythology*, which epitomizes older sources. Aslaug is the daughter of Iceland's great hero, Sigurd, and Iceland's great heroine, Brynhild, and her life is set down in this poem most beautifully. Again we note that the added touches of later poets fail to leave the sense of the strenuous in the picture. Aslaug is like a favorite representation of Brynhild that we have seen, a lily-maid in aspect, or a Marguerite. Her mother's masculinity is gone, and with it the Old Norse flavor. It is the privilege of our age to enjoy both the virility of the Old Norse and the delicacy of the mediaeval conceptions, and William Morris has caught both.

3.

In the opening lines of "The Fostering of Aslaug," our poet wrote his doubts about his ability to sing the life of Sigurd in be-fitting manner. At that time he said:

> But now have I no heart to raise
> That mighty sorrow laid asleep,
> That love so sweet, so strong and deep,
> That as ye hear the wonder told
> In those few strenuous words of old,
> The whole world seems to rend apart
> When heart is torn away from heart.

(Vol. III, p. 28.)

It is a common complaint against the poetry of William Morris that it is too long-winded. Each to his taste in this matter, but we beg to call attention to one line in the above passage:

> In those few strenuous words of old.

Whatever may have been Morris' tendency when he wrote his own poetry, he
knew when concision was a virtue in the poetry of others. There is no better description of the *Voelsunga Saga* than the above line, and William Morris gave the English people a literal version of the saga, if mayhap that strenuous paucity might translate the old spirit. But, as if he knew that many readers would fail to make much of this version, he tried again on a larger scale, and the great volume *Sigurd the Volsung*, epic in character and proportions, was the result. Of these two we shall now speak.

The *Voelsunga Saga* was published in 1870, only two years after Morris had begun to study Icelandic with Eirikr Magnusson. The latter's name is on the title page as the first of the two co-translators. The *Saga* was supplemented by certain songs from the *Elder Edda* which were introduced by the translators at points where they would come naturally in the story. The work, both in prose and verse, is well done, and the attempt was successful to make, as the preface proposes, the "rendering close and accurate, and, if it might be so, at the same time, not over prosaic." The last two paragraphs of this preface are particularly interesting to one who is tracing the influence of Old Norse literature on English literature, because they are words with power, that have stirred men and will stir men to learn more about a wonderful land and its lore. We copy them entire:

"As to the literary quality of this work we might say much, but we think we may well trust the reader of poetic insight to break through whatever entanglement of strange manners or unused element may at first trouble him, and to meet the nature and beauty with which it is filled: we cannot doubt that such a reader will be intensely touched by finding, amidst all its wildness and remoteness, such startling realism, such subtilty, such close sympathy with all the passions that may move himself to-day.

"In conclusion, we must again say how strange it seems to us, that this Volsung Tale, which is in fact an unversified poem, should never before have been translated into English. For this is the Great Story of the North, which should be to all our race what the Tale of Troy was to the Greeks--to all our race first, and afterwards, when the change of the world has made our race nothing more than a name of what has been--a story too--then should it be to those that come after us no less than the Tale of Troy has been to us."

Morris wrote a prologue in verse for this volume, and it is an exquisite poem, such as only he seemed able to indite. So often does the reader of Morris come upon gems like this, that one is tempted to rail against the common ignorance about him:

O hearken, ye who speak the English Tongue,
How in a waste land ages long ago,
The very heart of the North bloomed into song
After long brooding o'er this tale of woe!

.   .   .   .

Yea, in the first gray dawning of our race,
This ruth-crowned tangle to sad hearts was dear.

.   .   .   .

So draw ye round and hearken, English Folk,
Unto the best tale pity ever wrought!
Of how from dark to dark bright Sigurd broke,
Of Brynhild's glorious soul with love distraught,
Of Gudrun's weary wandering unto naught,
Of utter love defeated utterly,
Of Grief too strong to give Love time to die!

4.

Six years later, in 1877 (English edition), Morris published the long poem, *The Story of Sigurd the Volsung and The Fall of the Niblungs*, and in it gave the peerless crown of all English poems springing from Old Norse sources. The poet considered this his most important work, and he was prouder of it than of any other literary work that he did. One who studies it can understand this pride, but he cannot understand the neglect by the reading public of this remarkable poem. The history of book-selling in the last decade shows strange revivals of interest in authors long dead; it will be safe to prophesy such a revival for

William Morris, because valuable treasures will not always remain hidden. In his case, however, it will not be a revival, because there has not been an awakening yet. That awakening must come, and thousands will see that William Morris was a great poet who have not yet heard of his name. Let us look at his greatest work with some degree of minuteness.

The opening lines are a good model of the meter, and we find it different from any that we have considered so far. There are certain peculiarities about it that make it seem a perfect medium for translating the Old Norse spirit. Most of these peculiarities are in the opening lines, and so we may transfer them to this page:[32]

> There was a dwelling of Kings ere the world was waxen old;
> Dukes were the door-wards there, and the roofs were thatched with gold;
> Earls were the wrights that wrought it, and silver nailed its doors;
> Earls' wives were the weaving-women, queens' daughters strewed its floors,
> And the masters of its song-craft were the mightiest men that cast
> The sails of the storm of battle adown the bickering blast.

Everybody knows that alliteration was a principle of Icelandic verse. It strikes the ear that hears Icelandic poetry for the first time--or the eye that sees it, since most of us read it silently--as unpleasantly insistent, but on fuller acquaintance, we lose this sense of obtrusiveness. Morris, in this poem, uses alliteration, but so skilfully that only the reader that seeks it discovers it. A less superb artist would have made it stick out in every line, so that the device would be a hindrance to the story-telling. As it is, nowhere in the more than nine thousand lines of **Sigurd the Volsung** is this alliteration an excrescence, but everywhere it is woven into the grand design of a fabric which is the richer for its foreign workmanship.

Notice that **duke** and **battle** and **master** are the only words not thoroughly Teutonic. This overwhelming predominance of the Anglo-Saxon element over the French is in keeping with the original of the story. Of course it is an accident that so small a proportion of Latin derivatives is found in these six lines, but the fact remains that Morris set himself to tell a Teutonic story in Teutonic idiom. That idiom is not very strange to present-day readers, indeed we may say it has but a fillip of strangeness. Archaisms are characteristic of poetic diction, and those found in this poem that are not common to other poetry are used to gain an Old Norse flavor. The following words taken from Book I of the poem are the only unfamiliar ones: **benight**, meaning "at night"; "so **win** the long years over"; **eel-grig**; **sackless**; **bursten**, a participle. The compounds **door-ward** and **song-craft** are representative of others that are sprinkled in fair number through the poem. They are the best that our language can do to reproduce the fine combinations that the Icelandic language formed so readily. English lends itself well to this device, as the many compounds show that Morris took from common usage. Such words as **roof-tree**, **song-craft**, **empty-handed**, **grave-mound**, **store-house**, taken at random from the pages of this poem, show that the genius of our language permits such formations. When Morris carries the practice a little further, and makes for his poem such words as **door-ward**, **chance-hap**, **slumber-tide**, **troth-word**, **God-home**, and a thousand others, he is not taking liberties with the language, and he is using a powerful aid in translating the Old Norse spirit.

One more peculiar characteristic of Icelandic is admirably exhibited in this poem. We have seen that Warton recognized in the "Runic poets" a warmth of fancy which expressed itself in "circumlocution and comparisons, not as a matter of necessity, but of choice and skill." Certainly Morris in using these circumlocutions in **Sigurd the Volsung**, has exercised remarkable skill in weaving them into his story. Like the alliterations, they are part of an harmonious design. Examples abound, like:

> Adown unto the swan-bath the Volsung Children ride;

and this other for the same thing, the sea:

> While sleepeth the fields of the fishes amidst the summer-tide.

Still others for the water are **swan-mead**, and "bed-gear of the swan."

"The serpent of death" and **war-flame**, for sword; **earth-bone**, for rock; **fight-sheaves**, for armed hosts; **seaburg**, for boats, are other striking examples.

So much for the mechanical details of this poem. Its literary features are so exceptional that we must examine them at length.

Book I is entitled "Sigmund" and the description is set at the head of it. "In this book is told of the earlier days of the Volsungs, and of Sigmund the father of Sigurd, and of his deeds, and of how he died while Sigurd was yet unborn in his mother's womb."

There are many departures from the **Voelsunga Saga** in this poetic version, and all seem to be accounted for by a desire to impress present-day readers with this story. The poem begins with Volsung, omitting, therefore, the marvelous birth of that king and the oath of the unborn child to "flee in fear from neither fire nor the sword." The saga makes the wolf kill one of Volsung's sons every night; the poem changes the number to two. A magnificent scene is invented by Morris in the midnight visit of Signy to the wood where her brothers had been slain. She speaks to the brother that is left, desiring to know what he is doing:

O yea, I am living indeed, and this labor of mine hand
Is to bury the bones of the Volsungs; and lo, it is well nigh done.
So draw near, Volsung's daughter, and pile we many a stone
Where lie the gray wolf s gleanings of what was once so good.

(P. 23.)

The dialogue of brother and sister is a mighty conception, and surely
the old Icelanders would have called Morris a rare singer. Sigmund tells
the story of the deaths of his brothers, adding:

But now was I wroth with the Gods, that had made the Volsungs for
nought;
And I said: in the Day of their Doom a man's help shall they miss.

(P. 24.)

But Signy is reconciled to the workings of Fate:

I am nothing so wroth as thou art with the ways of death and hell,
For thereof had I a deeming when all things were seeming well.

The day to come shall set their woes right:

There as thou drawest thy sword, thou shall think of the days that were
And the foul shall still seem foul, and the fair shall still seem fair;
But thy wit shall then be awakened, and thou shalt know indeed
Why the brave man's spear is broken, and his war shield fails at need;
Why the loving is unbeloved; why the just man falls from his state;
Why the liar gains in a day what the soothfast strives for late.
Yea, and thy deeds shalt thou know, and great shall thy gladness be;
As a picture all of gold thy life-days shalt thou see,
And know that thou wert a God to abide through the hurry and haste;

A God in the golden hall, a God in the rain-swept waste,
A God in the battle triumphant, a God on the heap of the slain:
And thine hope shall arise and blossom, and thy love shall be quickened again:
And then shalt thou see before thee the face of all earthly ill;
Thou shalt drink of the cup of awakening that thine hand hath holpen to fill;
By the side of the sons of Odin shalt thou fashion a tale to be told
In the hall of the happy Baldur.

(P. 25.)

In this wise one Christian might hearten another to accept the dealings of Providence to-day. While we do not think that a worshipper of Odin would have spoken all these words, they are not an undue exaggeration of the noblest traits of the old Icelandic religion.

The poem does not record the death of Siggeir's and Signy's son, though the saga does. Morris adds a touch when he makes the imprisoned men exult over the sword that Signy drops into their grave, and he also puts into the mouth of Siggeir in the burning hall words that the saga does not contain. The poem says that the women of the Gothfolk were permitted to retire from the burning hall, but the saga has no such statement. The war of foul words between Granmar and Sinfjoetli is left in the saga, and the cause of Gudrod's death is changed from rivalry over a woman to anger over a division of war booty. In Sigmund's lament over his childlessness we have another of the poet's additions, and certainly we find no fault with the liberty:

The tree was stalwart, but its boughs are old and worn.
Where now are the children departed, that amidst my life were born?
I know not the men about me, and they know not of my ways:
I am nought but a picture of battle, and a song for the people to

praise.
I must strive with the deeds of my kingship, and yet when mine hour is
come
It shall meet me as glad as the goodman when he bringeth the last load
home.

(P. 56.)

When the great hero dies, Morris puts into his mouth another of the
magnificent speeches that are the glory of this poem. Four lines from it
must suffice:

When the gods for one deed asked me I ever gave them twain;
Spendthrift of glory I was, and great was my life-day's gain.

.   .   .   .
.   .

Our wisdom and valour have kissed, and thine eyes shall see the fruit,
And the joy for his days that shall be hath pierced my heart to the
root.

(P. 62.)

It appears from this study of Book I that **Sigurd the Volsung** has
adapted the saga story to our civilization and our art, holding to the
best of the old and supplementing it by new that is ever in keeping with
the old. Other instances of this eclectic habit may be seen in the other
three books, but we shall quote from these for other purposes.

Book II is entitled "Regin." "Now this is the first book of the life and
death of Sigurd the Volsung, and therein is told of the birth of him,
and of his dealings with Regin the Master of Masters, and of his deeds

in the waste places of the earth."

Morris was deeply read in Old Norse literature, and out of his stores of knowledge he brought vivifying details for this poem. Such, for instance, is the description of Sigurd's eyes, not found just here in the saga:

> In the bed there lieth a man-child, and his eyes look straight on the sun.

> .   .   .   .
> . .

> Yet they shrank in their rejoicing before the eyes of the child.

> .   .   .   .
> . .

In the naming of the child by an ancient name, the meaning of that name is indicated:

> O *Sigurd*, Son of the Volsungs, O Victory yet to be!

The festivities over the birth of the child are wonderfully described in the brief lines, and they are a picture out of another book than the saga:

> Earls think of marvellous stories, and along the golden strings
> Flit words of banded brethren and names of war-fain Kings.

Over and over again in this poem Morris records the Icelanders' desire "to leave a tale to tell," and here are Sigurd's words to Regin who has been egging him on to deeds:

Yet I know that the world is wide, and filled with deeds unwrought;
And for e'en such work was I fashioned, lest the songcraft come to nought,
When the harps of God-home tinkle, and the Gods are at stretch to hearken:
Lest the hosts of the Gods be scanty when their day hath begun to darken.

(P. 82.)

In Book II we have other great speeches that the poet has put into the mouth of his characters with little or no justification in the original saga. Chap. XIV of the saga contains Regin's tale of his brothers, and of the gold called "Andvari's Hoard," and that tale is severely brief and plain. The account in the poem is expanded greatly, and the conception of Regin materially altered. In the saga he was not the discontented youngest son of his father, prone to talk of his woes and to lament his lot. In the poem he does this in so eloquent a fashion that almost we are persuaded to sympathize with him. Certainly his lines were hard, to have outlived his great deeds, and to hear his many inventions ascribed to the gods. The speech of the released Odin to Reidmar is modeled on Job's conception of omnipotence, and it is one of the memorable parts of this book. Gripir's prophecy, too, is a majestic work, and its original was three sentences in the saga and the poem *Gripisspa* in the heroic songs of the *Edda*. Here Morris rises to the heights of Sigurd's greatness:

Sigurd, Sigurd! O great, O early born!
O hope of the Kings first fashioned! O blossom of the morn!
Short day and long remembrance, fair summer of the North!
One day shall the worn world wonder how first thou wentest forth!

(P. 111.)

Those who have read William Morris know that he is a master of nature description. The "Glittering Heath" offered a fine opportunity for this sort of work, and in this piece we have another departure from the saga. Morris made hundreds of pictures in this poem, but the pages describing the journey to the "Glittering Heath" are packed with them to an extraordinary degree. Here is Iceland in very fact, all dust and ashes to the eye:

> More changeless than mid-ocean, as fruitless as its floor.

We confess that there is something in the scene that holds us, all shorn of beauty though it is. We do not want to go the length of Thomas Hardy, however, who, in that wonderful first chapter of *The Return of the Native* has a similar heath to describe. "The new vale of Tempe," says he, "may be a gaunt waste in Thule: human souls may find themselves in closer and closer harmony with external things wearing a sombreness distasteful to our race when it was young.... The time seems near, if it has not actually arrived, when the mournful sublimity of a moor, a sea, or a mountain, will be all of nature that is absolutely consonant with the moods of the more thinking among mankind. And ultimately, to the commonest tourist, spots like Iceland may become what the vineyards and myrtlegardens of South Europe are to him now." Is it not a suggestive thought that England and the nineteenth century evolved a pessimism which poor Iceland on its ash-heap never could conceive? William Morris was an Icelander, not an Englishman, in his philosophy.

In this same scene, a notable deviation from the saga is the conversation between Regin and Sigurd concerning the relations that shall be between them after the slaying of Fafnir. Here Morris impresses the lesson of Regin's greed, taking the un-Icelandic device of preaching to serve his purpose:

Let it lead thee up to heaven, let it lead thee down to hell,
The deed shall be done tomorrow: thou shalt have that measureless Gold,
And devour the garnered wisdom that blessed thy realm of old,
That hath lain unspent and begrudged in the, very heart of hate:
With the blood and the might of thy brother thine hunger shalt thou
sate:
And this deed shall be mine and thine; but take heed for what followeth
then!

(P. 119.)

In still another place has Morris departed far from the saga story.
According to the poem, Sigurd meets each warning of Fafnir that the gold
will be the curse of its possessor with the assurance that he will cast
the gold abroad, and let none of it cling to his fingers. The saga,
however, has this very frank confession: "Home would I ride and lose all
that wealth, if I deemed that by the losing thereof I should never die;
but every brave and true man will fain have his hand on wealth till that
last day." Here, again, we see an adaptation of the story of the poem to
modern conceptions of nobility. It remains to be said that the ernes
move Sigurd to take the gold for the gladdening of the world, and they
assure him that a son of the Volsung had nought to fear from the Curse.
The seven-times-repeated "Bind the red rings, O Sigurd," is an admirable
poem, but it does not contain information concerning Brynhild, as do the
strophes of *Reginsmal* which are the model for this lay.

Let us look at the art of Morris as it is shown in telling "How Sigurd
awoke Brynhild upon Hindfell." As in the saga, so in the English poem,
this incident has a setting most favorable to the display of its
remarkable beauties. It is a picture as pure and sweet as it has ever
entered into the mind of man to conceive. The conception belongs to the
poetic lore of many nations, and children are early introduced to the

story of "Sleeping Beauty." There are some features of the Old Norse version that are especially charming, and first among them is the address of the awakened Brynhild to the sun and the earth. We are told that this maiden loved the radiant hero that here awoke her from her age-long sleep, but not for him is her first greeting. A finer thrill moves her than love for a man, and in Morris's poem, this feeling finds singularly beautiful expression:

> All hail O Day and thy Sons, and thy kin of the coloured things!
> Hail, following Night, and thy Daughter that leadeth thy wavering wings!
> Look down with unangry eyes on us today alive,
> And give us the hearts victorious, and the gain for which we strive!
> All hail, ye Lords of God-home, and ye Queens of the House of Gold!
> Hail thou dear Earth that bearest, and thou Wealth of field and fold!
> Give us, your noble children, the glory of wisdom and speech,
> And the hearts and the hands of healing, and the mouths and hands that teach!

(P. 140.)

In order to see just what the art of Morris has done for this poem, let us compare this address with the rendering of the ***Sigrdrifumal***, which tell the same story and which Morris and Magnusson have incorporated into their translation of the ***Voelsunga Saga***. The verses are not in the original saga:

> Hail to the day come back!
> Hail, sons of the daylight!
> Hail to thee, dark night, and thy daughter!
> Look with kind eyes a-down,
> On us sitting here lonely,
> And give unto us the gain that we long for.

Hail to the AEsir,
And the sweet Asyniur!
Hail to the fair earth fulfilled of plenty!
Fair words, wise hearts,
Would we win from you,
And healing hands while life we hold.

To get the full benefit of the comparison of the old and the new, let us set in conjunction with these versions a severely literal translation of the *Edda* strophes themselves:

Hail, O Day,
Hail, O Sons of the Day,
Hail Night and kinswoman!
With unwroth eyes
look on us here
and give to us sitting ones victory.
Hail, O Gods,
Hail, O Goddesses,
Hail, O bounteous Earth!
Speech and wisdom
give to us, the excellent twain,
and healing hands during life.

These stages in the progress of the gold from mine to mint furnish their own commentary. The finished product will pass current with the most exacting of assayers, as well as gladden the hearts of the poor one whose hand seldom touches gold.

If the skill of the poet in this case have merited resemblance to that of the refiner of gold, what name less than alchemy can characterize his achievement in the rest of this scene? From the first words of Brynhild's life-story:

I am she that loveth; I was born of the earthly folk;

to the tender words that tell of the coming of another day:

And fresh and all abundant abode the deeds of Day,

there is a succession of beautiful scenes and glorious speeches such as only a master of magic could have gotten out of the original story. The Eddaic account of the Valkyr's disobedience to All-Father, pictures a saucy and self-willed maiden. Sentence has been pronounced upon her, and thus the story continues: "But I said I would vow a vow against it, and marry no man that knew fear." The ***Voelsunga Saga*** gives exactly the same account, but the poetic version of Morris saves the maiden for our respect and admiration. It is not effrontery, but repentance that speaks in the voice of Brynhild here:

The thoughts of my heart overcame me, and the pride of my wisdom and speech,
And I scorned the earth-folk's Framer, and the Lord of the world I must teach.

In the Icelandic version, Odin makes no speech at the dooming, but Morris puts into his mouth this magnificent address:

And he cried: "Thou hast thought in thy folly that the Gods have friends and foes,
That they wake, and the world wends onward, that they sleep, and the world slips back,
That they laugh, and the world's weal waxeth, that they frown and fashion the wrack:
Thou hast cast up the curse against me; it shall aback on thine head;
Go back to the sons of repentance, with the children of sorrow wed!

For the Gods are great unholpen, and their grief is seldom seen,
And the wrong that they will and must be is soon as it hath not been."

(P. 141.)

Morris has here again exercised the poet's privilege of adding to the
story that was the pride of an entire age, in order to serve his own the
better. If he was wise in these additions, he was no less wise in
subtractions and in preservations. The saga has a long address by
Brynhild, opening with mystical advice concerning the power of runes,
and closing grandly with wise words that sound like a page from the Old
Testament. The former find no place in **Sigurd the Volsung**, but the
latter are turned into mighty phrases that wonderfully preserve the
spirit of the original.

One passage more from Book II:

So they climb the burg of Hindfell, and hand in hand they fare,
Till all about and above them is nought but the sunlit air,
And there close they cling together rejoicing in their mirth;
For far away beneath them lie the kingdoms of the earth,
And the garths of men-folk's dwellings and the streams that water them,
And the rich and plenteous acres, and the silver ocean's hem,
And the woodland wastes and the mountains, and all that holdeth all;
The house and the ship and the island, the loom and the mine and the
stall,
The beds of bane and healing, the crafts that slay and save,
The temple of God and the Doom-ring, the cradle and the grave.

(P. 145.)

These ten lines serve to illustrate very well one of the most remarkable
powers of Morris. Just consider for a moment the number of details that

are crowded into this picture, and then notice how few are the strokes required to put them there. For this rapid painting of a crowded canvas Morris is second to none among English poets. This power to put a whole landscape or a complex personality into a few lines is the direct outcome of his study of Old Norse literature. Icelandic poetry is characterized by this quality. One has but to compare the account of the end of the world as it is found in the last strophes of *Voeluspa*, or in the *Prose Edda*, with the similar account in *Revelations* to see how much two languages may differ in this respect. It would seem as if the short verses characteristic of Icelandic poetry forbade lengthy descriptions. The effect must be produced by a number of quick strokes: there is never time to go over a line once made. A simile is never elaborated, a new one is made when the poet wishes to insist on the figure. Take the second strophe of the "Ancient Lay of Gudrun" as an example, in the translation by Morris and Magnusson:

> Such was my Sigurd
> Among the Sons of Giuki
> As is the green leek
> O'er the low grass waxen,
> Or a hart high-limbed
> Over hurrying deer,
> Or gleed-red gold
> Over grey silver.

That is the Icelandic fashion; William Morris has caught it in the *Story of Sigurd*. Matthew Arnold has not seen fit to use it in his "Balder Dead," as these lines show:

> Him the blind Hoder met, as he came up
> From the sea cityward, and knew his step;
> Nor yet could Hermod see his brother's face,
> For it grew dark; but Hermod touched his arm.

And as a spray of honeysuckle flowers
Brushes across a tired traveller's face
Who shuffles thro the deep-moistened dust,
On a May-evening, in the darkened lanes,
And starts him that he thinks a ghost went by--
So Hoder brushed by Hermod's side.

These are noble lines, but altogether foreign to Icelandic.

Book III opens with the dream of Gudrun and Brynhild's interpretation of it. This matter is managed in accordance with our own standards of art, and thus differs materially from the saga story. In the latter a most naive procedure is adopted, for Brynhild prophesies that Sigurd shall leave her for Gudrun, through Grimhild's guile, that strife shall come between them, and that Sigurd shall die and Gudrun wed Atli. The whole later story is thus revealed. This is not a story-teller's art, but it sets clear the Old Norse acceptance of fate's dealings. Of course Morris' poetic action explains the dream perfectly, but the details are not so frankly given.

"Thou shalt live and love and lose, and mingle in murder and war," is the gist of Brynhild's message, and the whole future history is there.

This poem has often been called an epic, and certainly there are many epical characteristics in it. One of them is the recurrence of certain formulas, and in Books III and IV these are rather more abundant than in the first two books. Thus the sword of Sigurd is praised in the same words, again and again:

It hath not its like in the heavens nor has earth of its fellow told.

Then, there is the "cloudy hall-roof" of the Niblungs. Gudrun is "the white-armed"; Grimhild is "the wisest of women"; Hogni is the "wise-heart"; the Niblungs are "the Cloudy People"; their beds are "blue-covered"; "the Godson the hangings" is an expression that recurs very often, and it recalls the fact that Morris was an artisan as well as an artist.

In the preceding books we have noted that Morris lengthened the saga story in his poem by the introduction of speeches that find no place in the original. In this book we see another lengthening process, which, with that already noted, goes far to account for the difference in bulk between the saga and the poem. Chap. XXVI of the saga, tells in less than a thousands words how Sigurd comes to the Giukings and is wedded to Gudrun. His reception is told in one hundred words; his abode with the Giukings is set forth in even fewer words; Grimhild's plotting and administering of the drugged drink are told in two hundred words; his acceptance of Gudrun's hand and her brother's allegiance are as tersely pictured; kingdoms are conquered, a son is born to Sigurd, and Grimhild plots to have Sigurd get Brynhild for her son Gunnar, yet the record of it all is compressed within one hundred and fifty words. Of course, the modern poet can hem himself within no such narrow bounds as this. The artistic value of these various incidents is priceless, and Morris has lingered upon them lovingly and long. He spreads the story over forty pages, or a thousand lines, and I avow, after a third reading of these three sections of the poem, that I would spare no line of them. How we love this Sigurd of the poet's painting! And what a noble gospel he proclaims to the Giukings:

> For peace I bear unto thee, and to all the kings of the earth,
> Who bear the sword aright, and are crowned with the crown of worth;
> But unpeace to the lords of evil, and the battle and the death;
> And the edge of the sword to the traitor, and the flame to the
> slanderous breath:
> And I would that the loving were loved, and I would that the weary
> should sleep,

And that man should hearken to man, and that he that soweth should reap.

(P. 174.)

Here, by the way, is the burden of Morris's preaching in the cause of a better society. It recurs a few pages further on in the poem, where the Niblungs bestow praise on this new hero:

> And they say, when the sun of summer shall come aback to the land,
> It shall shine on the fields of the tiller that fears no heavy hand;
> That the sleep shall be for the plougher, and the loaf for him that sowed,
> Through every furrowed acre where the Son of Sigmund rode.

(P. 178.)

It need hardly be remarked that this Sigurd is not the sagaman's ideal. The Icelanders never evolved such high conceptions of man's obligations to man, but in their ignorance they were no worse off than their continental brethren, for these forgot their greatest Teacher's teaching, and modern social science must point them back to it.

This Sigurd that we love becomes the Sigurd that we pity in the drinking of a draught. Sorrow takes the place of joy in his life, and "the soul is changed in him," so that men may say that on this day they saw him die the first time, who was to die a second time by Guttorm's sword. Gloom spreads over all the earth with the quenching of Sigurd's joy:

> In the deedless dark he rideth, and all things he remembers save one,
> And nought else hath he care to remember of all the deeds he hath done.

Here is illustrated the essential difference between the sagaman's art and the modern story-teller's. The Icelander must tell his story in haste; the deeds of men are his care, not their divagations nor their psychologizings. The modern writer must linger on every step in the story until the motive and the meaning are laid bare. In the present-day version Sigurd's mental sufferings are described at length, and our hearts are wrung at his unmerited woes. The saga knows no such woes, and to all appearance Sigurd's life is not unhappy to its very end. Indeed, it appears in more than one place in Morris's poem that Sigurd has become godlike through the hard experiences of his life. Take this passage as an illustration:

> So is Sigurd yet with the Niblungs, and he loveth Gudrun his wife,
> And wendeth afield with the brethren to the days of the dooming of life;
> And nought his glory waneth, nor falleth the flood of praise:
> To every man he hearkeneth, nor gainsayeth any grace,
> And, glad is the poor in the Doom-ring when he seeth his face mid the Kings,
> For the tangle straighteneth before him, and the maze of crooked things.
> But the smile is departed from him, and the laugh of Sigurd the young,
> And of few words now is he waxen, and his songs are seldom sung.
> Howbeit of all the sad-faced was Sigurd loved the best;
> And men say: Is the king's heart mighty beyond all hope of rest?
> Lo, how he beareth the people! how heavy their woes are grown!
> So oft were a God mid the Goth-folk, if he dwelt in the world alone.

(P. 205.)

Set this by the side of the saga: "This is truer," says Sigurd, "that I loved thee better than myself, though I fell into the wiles from whence our lives may not escape; for whenso my own heart and mind availed me, then I sorrowed sore that thou wert not my wife; but as I might I put my trouble from me, for in a king's dwelling was I; and withal and in spite of all I was well content that we were all together. Well may it be, that that shall come to pass which is foretold; neither shall I fear the fulfilment thereof." (***Voelunga Saga***, Chap. XXIX.) These words are spoken to Brynhild after she has discovered what she regards as Sigurd's treachery. His words are dictated by a noble resignation to fate, but his very next remark shows a moral meanness not at all in keeping with Morris's conception. Sigurd said: "This my heart would, that thou and I should go into one bed together; even so wouldst thou be my wife."

There have been many griefs depicted in this poem, but surely here are set forth the most pitiless of them all. The guile-won Brynhild travels in state to the Cloudy Hall of the Niblungs, and the whole people come out to meet her. They are astonished at her beauty, and give her cordial greeting and welcome to her husband's house. Proud and majestic, the marvelous woman steps from her golden wain, and gives friendly but passionless greeting to Gunnar as she places her hand in his. For each of Gunnar's brothers she has a kindly word, as she has for Grimhild, too. She asks to see the foster-brother of whom such wondrous tales are told, and whose name she heard from Gunnar's lips with never a tremor--"Sigurd, the Volsung, the best man ever born." Grimhild stands between them for a time, but the meeting has to come. Then Brynhild remembers, and Sigurd sees the unveiled past:

> Her heart ran back through the years, and yet her lips did move
> With the words she spake on Hindfell, when they plighted troth of love.

> .   .   .   .
> .   .   .

> His face is exceeding glorious and awful to behold;
> For of all his sorrow he knoweth and his hope smit dead and cold:

.   .   .   .

.   .   .

For the will of the Norns is accomplished, and outworn is Grimhild's spell
And nought now shall blind or help him, and the tale shall be to tell.

(P. 226.)

There's the note of the whole history--the will of the Norns and the note of a whole Northern literature, as it is of a whole Southern literature. Man, the puppet, in the hands of Fate; however man may think and reason and assure himself that the dispensation of Fate is just, the supreme moment of realization will always be a tragedy:

He hath seen the face of Brynhild, and he knows why she hath come,
And that his is the hand that hath drawn her to the Cloudy People's home:
He knows of the net of the days, and the deeds that the Gods have bid,
And no whit of the sorrow that shall be from his wakened soul is hid.

(P. 226.)

In such an hour, what are conquests of a glorious past, what are honors, crowns, loves, hates? The mind can think of little matters only:

His heart speeds back to Hindfell, and the dawn of the wakening day;
And the hours betwixt are as nothing, and their deeds are fallen away.

(P. 226.)

Is aught to be said to one in such a crisis, the words are weak and commonplace. There is Brynhild's greeting to Sigurd:

> If aught thy soul shall desire while yet thou livest on earth,
> I pray that thou mayst win it, nor forget its might and worth.

The shattered mind of Sigurd tries to grasp the meaning of the harmless words, and like common sounds that are so fearful in the night, the phrases assume a terrible import:

> All grief, sharp scorn, sore longing, stark death in her voice he knew.

Then again conies the dominant note of this story:

> Gone forth is the doom of the Norns, and what shall be answer thereto,
> While the death that amendeth lingers?

Here is a hint of the end of all--"the death that amendeth," and from this point to the end of the story there is no gleam of happiness for anyone.

Book IV brings to a majestic close this mighty history. We have dwelt so long on the wonderful poetry of the other books that we must refrain from further comment in this strain. As we read these eloquent imaginings, we regret that the English reading public have left this work through fear of its great length or the ignorance of its existence, in the dust of half-forgotten shelves. Gold disused is true gold none the less, and the ages to come may be more appreciative than the present.

For the sake of rounding out this story, be it noted concerning this Book IV, that the poet has taken liberties with the saga story here, as elsewhere. Motives more easily understood in our day are assigned for the deeds of dread that throng these closing scenes. Gudrun weds King

Atli at her mother's bidding, and under the influence of a wicked potion, but neither mother nor magic drives the memory of Sigurd from her mind. She lives to bring destruction upon her husband's murderers, and those murderers are her own flesh and blood. Through her appeals to Atli's greed, and through Knefrud's lies in the Niblung court, the visit of her proud brothers to her pliant husband is brought about. The saga makes Atli the arch-plotter, and the motive his desire to possess the gold. This sentence exculpates Gudrun from any wrong intention towards her brothers: "Now the queen wots of their conspiring, and misdoubts her that this would mean some beguiling of her brethren." (Chap. XXXIV.) In Chap. XXXVIII, we are told that Gudrun fights on the side of her brothers. We see at once the superiority of the poet's motive for a modern tragedy.

It is impressed upon the reader of an epic that the plan of its maker does not call for fine analysis of character. The epic poet is concerned necessarily with large considerations, and his personages do not split hairs from the south to the southeast side. One sign of this is seen in the epic formulae employed to characterize the personages of the story. Such formulas are in *Sigurd the Volsung* in abundance, as we have noted on another page. But there are also many departures from the epic model in this poem. Some of these we have referred to in the remarks on Book III, where we noted Sigurd's mental sufferings. In Book IV we have a discrimination of character that is not epic, but dramatic in its minuteness. In the speech and the deeds of the Niblungs their pride and selfishness is clearly set forth, but the individual members of that race are distinguished by traits very minutely drawn. Thus Hogni is the wary Niblung, and is averse to accepting Atli's invitation:

> "I know not, I know not," said Hogni, "but an unsure bridge is the sea,
> And such would I oft were builded betwixt my foeman and me.
> I know a sorrow that sleepeth, and a wakened grief I know,
> And the torment of the mighty is a strong and fearful foe."

(P. 281.)

Gunnar is here distinguished as a hypocrite by word and deed; Gudrun remembers Sigurd in her exile and schemes and plots to make her husband Atli work her vengeance on the Niblungs; Atli is greedy for gold and Gudrun's task is not hard; Knefrud is a liar whose words are winning, and overcome the scruples of the Niblungs. In these careful discriminations of character we see a non-epical trait, and of necessity therefore, a non-Icelandic trait. The sagaman was epic in his tone.

As a last appreciation of the art of William Morris as it is displayed in this poem, we would call attention to the tremendous battle-piece entitled "Of the Battle in Atli's Hall." It is the climax of this marvelous poem, and in no detail is it inadequate to its place in the work. The poet's constructive power is here demonstrated to be of the highest order, and in the majestic sweep of events that is here depicted, we see the poet in his original role of *maker*. The sagaman's skill had not the power to conceive this titanic drama, and the memory of his battle-piece is quite effaced by the modern invention. In blood and fire the story comes to an end with Gudrun,

    The white and silent woman above the slaughter set.

As we turn from the scene and the book, that figure fades not away. And it is fitting that the last memory of this poem should be a picture of love and hate, inextricably bound together, for that is the irony of Fate, and Fate was mistress of the Old Norseman's world.

5.

Between the great works dealt with in the last two sections, which belong together and were therefore so considered, came the book of 1875, bearing the title ***Three Northern Love Stories and Other Tales***. It is as good a representation as Iceland can make in the love-story class.

These tales are charmingly told in the translation of Morris and Magnusson, the second one, "Frithiof the Bold," being a master-piece in its kind. Men will dare much for the love of a woman, and that is why the sagaman records love episodes at all. Frithiof's voyage to the Orkneys in Chap. VI is a stormpiece that vies with anything of its kind in modern literature. It is Norse to the core, and we love the peerless young hero who forgets not his manhood in his chagrin of defeat at love. Surely there is fitness in these outbursts of song in moments of extreme exultation or despair! "And he sang withal:

> "Helgi it is that helpeth
> The white-head billows' waxing;
> Cold time unlike the kissing
> In the close of Baldur's Meadow!
> So is the hate of Helgi
> To that heart's love she giveth.
> O would that here I held her,
> Gift high above all giving!"

Modern literature has lost this conventionality of the older writings, found in Hebrew as well as in Icelandic, and we think it has lost something valuable. Morris thought so, too, for he restored the interpolated song-snatches in his Romances. We are tempted to dwell on these three love-stories, they are so fine; but we must leave them with the remark that they show the poet's appreciation of the worth of a foreign literature, and his great desire to have his countrymen share in his admiration for them. "The Story of Gunnlaug the Worm-Tongue and Raven the Skald," and "The Story of Viglund the Fair," are the other two stories that give the title to the volume, representing the thirteenth and fifteenth centuries, as "Frithiof" represented the fourteenth.

6.

With ***Sigurd the Volsung*** ended the first great Icelandic period of Morris's work. More than a dozen years passed before he returned to the field, and from 1889 until his death, in 1896, everything he wrote bore proofs of his abiding interest in and affection for the ancient literature. The remarkable series of romances, ***The House of the Wolfings*** (1889), ***The Roots of the Mountains*** (1890), ***The Story of the Glittering Plain*** (1891), ***The Wood Beyond the World*** (1895), ***The Well at the World's End*** (1896) and ***The Sundering Flood*** (posthumous), are none of them distinctively Old Norse in geography or in story, but they all have the flavor of the saga-translations, and are all the better for it. They are as original and as beautiful as the poet's tapestries and furniture, and if they did not provoke imitation as did the tapestries and furniture, it was not because they were not worth imitating: more than likely there were no imitators equal to the task. In these romances we have men and women with the characteristics of an olden time that are most worthy of conservation in the present time. The ideals of womanfolk and manfolk in ***The House of the Wolfings*** and ***The Roots of the Mountains***, for instance, are such as an Englishman might well be proud to have in his remote ancestry. Hall-Sun, Wood-Sun, Sunbeam, and Bowmay are wholesome women to meet in a story, and Thiodolf, Gold-mane, Iron-face and Hallward are every inch men for book-use or to commune with every day. Weaklings, too, abide in these stories, and Penny-thumb and Rusty and Fiddle and Wood-grey lend humanity to the company.

The two romances last mentioned are so steeped in the atmosphere of the sagas, that what with folk-motes and shut-beds, and byres, and man-quellers, and handsels and speech-friends, we seem to lose ourselves in yet another version of a northern tale. Morris retains the old idiom that he invented for his translations, and keeps the tyro thumbing his dictionary, but the charm is increased by the archaisms. As one seeks the words in the dictionary, one learns that Chaucer, Spenser and the Ballads were the wells from which he drew these rare words, and that his employment of them is only another phase of his love for the old far-off things. It is true that the language of Morris is not of any one stadium of English, but it is a poet's privilege to draw upon all history for his words as well as for his allusions, and the revivals in question are of worthy words pushed aside by the press of newer, but not necessarily better forms.

These works are the kind that show the influence of Old Norse literature as spiritual rather than substantial. The stories are not drawn from the older literature, nor are the settings patterned after it; but the impulses that swayed men and women in the sagaman's tale, and the motives that uplifted them, are found here. We cannot think that the English people will always be unmindful of the great debt that they owe to the Muse of the North.

7.

In 1891, Morris engaged in a literary enterprise that set the fashion for similar enterprises in succeeding years. With Eirikr Magnusson he undertook the making of ***The Saga Library***, "addressed to the whole reading public, and not only to students of Scandinavian history, folk-lore and language."[33] With Bernard Quaritch's imprint on the title pages, these volumes to the number of five were issued in exceptional type and form. The munificence of the publisher was equalled by the skill of the translators, and in their versions of "Howard, the Halt," "The Banded Men," and "Hen Thorir" (in Vol. I, dated 1891), "The Ere-Dwellers" (in Vol. II, dated 1892) and *Heimskringla* (in Vols. III, IV and V, dated 1893-4-5), the definitive translations of sterling sagas were given. As was the case with their *Grettis Saga*, the works rise to the dignity of masterpieces, and had we no other legacy from Morris' wealth of Icelandic scholarship, these translations were precious enough to keep us grateful through many generations.

8.

One more contribution to English literature hailing from the North, and we have done with William Morris's splendid gifts. The volume of 1891, entitled *Poems by the Way*, contains several pieces that must be reckoned with. The vividest recollections of Icelandic materials here made use of are the poems "Iceland First Seen," and "To the Muses of the North." No reader of the poet's biography can forget the remarkable journey that Morris made through Iceland, nor how he prepared for that journey with all the care and love of a pilgrim bound for a shrine of his deepest devotion. Every foot of ground was visited that had been hallowed by the noble souls and inspiring deeds of the past, and that pilgrimage warmed him to loving literary creation through the remainder of his life. The last two stanzas of the first of the poems just mentioned show what a strong hold the forsaken island had upon his affections, and go far to explain the success of his Icelandic work:

> O Queen of the grief without knowledge,
> of the courage that may not avail,
> Of the longing that may not attain,

of the love that shall never forget,
More joy than the gladness of laughter
thy voice hath amidst of its wail:
More hope than of pleasure fulfilled
amidst of thy blindness is set;
More glorious than gaining of all
thine unfaltering hand that shall fail:
For what is the mark on thy brow
but the brand that thy Brynhild doth bear?
Lone once, and loved and undone
by a love that no ages outwear.

Ah! when thy Balder conies back,
and bears from the heart of the Sun
Peace and the healing of pain,
and the wisdom that waiteth no more;
And the lilies are laid on thy brow
'mid the crown of the deeds thou hast done;
And the roses spring up by thy feet
that the rocks of the wilderness wore.
Ah! when thy Balder comes back
and we gather the gains he hath won,
Shall we not linger a little
to talk of thy sweetness of old,
Yea, turn back awhile to thy travail
whence the Gods stood aloof to behold?

In several other poems in this volume he recurs to the practice of his
romances, Scandinavianizes where the tendency of other poets would be
to mediaevalize. "Of the Wooing of Hallbiorn the Strong," and "The Raven
and the King's Daughter" are examples. Here we have ballads like those
that Coleridge and Keats conceived on occasion, full of the beauty that
lends itself so kindly to painted-glass decoration; clustered

spear-shafts, crested helms and curling banners, and everywhere lily hands combing yellow hair or broidering silken standards. But the names strike a strange note in these songs of Morris, and the accompaniments are very different from the mediaeval kind:

> Come ye carles of the south country,
> Now shall we go our kin to see!
> For the lambs are bleating in the south,
> And the salmon swims towards Olfus mouth.
> Girth and graithe and gather your gear!
> And ho for the other Whitewater![34]

The introduction of the homely arts of bread-winning distinguishes the romance of Scandinavia from the romance of Southern Europe, and here Morris struck into a new field for poetry. Wherever we turn to note the effects of Icelandic tradition, we find this presence of daily toil, always associated with dignity, never apologized for. The connection between Morris' art and Morris' socialism is not hard to explain.

No commentary can equal Morris' own poem, "To the Muse of the North," in setting forth the charm that drew him to the literature of Iceland:

> O Muse that swayest the sad Northern Song,
> Thy right hand full of smiting and of wrong,
> Thy left hand holding pity; and thy breast
> Heaving with hope of that so certain rest:
> Thou, with the grey eyes kind and unafraid,
> The soft lips trembling not, though they have said
> The doom of the World and those that dwell therein.
> The lips that smile not though thy children win
> The fated Love that draws the fated Death.
> O, borne adown the fresh stream of thy breath,
> Let some word reach my ears and touch my heart,

That, if it may be, I may have a part
In that great sorrow of thy children dead
That vexed the brow, and bowed adown the head,
Whitened the hair, made life a wondrous dream,
And death the murmur of a restful stream,
But left no stain upon those souls of thine
Whose greatness through the tangled world doth shine.
O Mother, and Love and Sister all in one,
Come thou; for sure I am enough alone
That thou thine arms about my heart shouldst throw,
And wrap me in the grief of long ago.

V.

IN THE LATTER DAYS.

ECHOES OF ICELAND IN LATER POETS.

After William Morris the northern strain that we have been listening for
in the English poets seems feeble and not worth noting. Nevertheless, it
must be remarked that in the harp of a thousand strings that wakes to
music under the bard's hands, there is a sweep which thrills to the
ancient traditions of the Northland. Now and then the poet reaches for
these strings, and gladdens us with some reminiscence of

old, unhappy, far-off things
And battles long ago.

As had already been intimated, the table of contents in a present-day volume of poetry is very apt to show an Old Norse title. Thus Robert Lord Lytton's ***Poems Historical and Characteristic*** (London, 1877) reveals among the poems on European, Oriental, classic and mediaeval subjects, "The Death of Earl Hacon," a strong piece inspired by an incident in ***Heimskringla***. In Robert Buchanan's multifarious versifying occurs this title: "Balder the Beautiful, A Song of Divine Death," but only the title is Old Norse; nothing in the poem suggests that origin except a notion or two of the end of all things. "Hakon" is the title of a short virile piece more nearly of the Norse spirit. Sidney Dobell's drama ***Balder*** has only the title to suggest the Icelandic, but Gerald Massey has the true ring in a number of lyrics, with themes drawn from the records of Norway's relations with England. In "The Norseman" there is a trumpet strain that recalls the best of the border-ballads; there is also a truthfulness of portraiture that argues a poet's, intuition in Gerald Massey, if not an acquaintance with the sagas:

> The Norseman's King must stand up tall,
> If he would be head over all;
> Mainmast of Battle! when the plain
> Is miry-red with bloody rain!
> And grip his weapon for the fight,
> Until his knuckles grin tooth-white,
> The banner-staff he bears is best
> If double handful for the rest:
> When "follow me" cries the Norseman.

He knows the gentler side of Old Norse character, too, a side which, as we have seen, was not suspected till Carlyle came:

> He hides at heart of his rough life,
> A world of sweetness for the Wife;

From his rude breast a Babe may press
Soft milk of human tenderness,--
Make his eyes water, his heart dance,
And sunrise in his countenance:
In merriest mood his ale he quaffs
By firelight, and with jolly heart laughs
The blithe, great-hearted Norseman.

The poem "Old King Hake," is as strikingly true in characterization as the preceding. In half a dozen strophes Massey has told a whole saga, and has found time, too, to describe "an iron hero of Norse mould." How miserable a personage is the Italian that flits through Browning's pages when contrasted with this hero:

When angry, out the blood would start
With old King Hake;
Not sneak in dark caves of the heart,
Where curls the snake,
And secret Murder's hiss is heard
Ere the deed be done:
He wove no web of wile and word;
He bore with none.
When sharp within its sheath asleep
Lay his good sword,
He held it royal work to keep
His kingly word.
A man of valour, bloody and wild,
In Viking need;
And yet of firelight feeling mild
As honey-mead.

Another poem, "The Banner-Bearer of King Olaf," pictures the strong fighter in a death he rejoiced to die. It is a good poem of the class that nerves men to die for the flag, and it has the Old Norse spirit. These poems are all from Massey's volume *My Lyrical Life* (London. 1889).

A glance at the other poems in Gerald Massey's volumes shows that like Morris, and like Kingsley, and like Carlyle, the poet was a workman eager to do for the workman. Is it not suggestive that these men found themselves drawn to Old Norse character and life? The Icelandic republic cherished character as the highest quality of citizenship, and put few or no social obstacles in the way of its achievement. The literature inspired by that life reveals a fellowship among the members of that republic that is the envy of social reformers of the present day. Morris makes one of the personages in *The Story of the Glittering Plain* (Chap. I) say these words: "And as for Lord, I knew not this word, for here dwell we the Sons of the Raven in good fellowship, with our wives that we have wedded, and our mothers who have borne us, and our sisters who serve us." Almost may this description serve for Iceland in its golden age, and so it is no wonder that the socialist, the priest, and the philosopher of our own disjointed times go back to the sagas for ideals to serve their countrymen.

We have no other poets to mention by name in connection with this Old Norse influence, although doubtless a search through the countless volumes that the presses drop into a cold and uncaring world would reveal other poems with Scandinavian themes. We close this section of our investigation with the remark already made, that, in the tables of titles in volumes of contemporary verse, acknowledgment to Old Norse poetry and prose are not the rarity they once were, and in poems of any kind allusions to the same sources are very common.

RECENT TRANSLATIONS.

We have already noted the beginning of serial publications of saga translations, namely, Morris and Magnusson's *Saga Library* which was stopped by the death of Morris when the fifth volume had been completed. By the last decade of the nineteenth century Icelandic had become one of the languages that an ordinary scholar might boast, and in consequence the list of translations began to lengthen very fast. Several English publishers with scholarly instincts were attracted to this field, and so the reading public may get at the sagas that were so long the exclusive possession of learned professors. *The Northern Library*, published by David Nutt, of London, already contains four volumes and more are promised: *The Saga of King Olaf Tryggwason,* by J. Sephton, appeared in 1895; *The Tale of Thrond of Gate* (*Faereyinga Saga*), by F. York Powell, in 1896; *Hamlet in Iceland* (*Ambales Saga*), by Israel Gollancz, in 1898; *The Saga of King Sverri of Norway* (*Sverris Saga*), by J. Sephton, in 1899. If we cannot give to these the praise of being great literature though translations, we can at least foresee that this process of turning all the readable sagas into English will quicken adaptations and increase the stock of allusions in modern writings.

An example of the publishers' feeling that the reading public will find an interest in the saga itself, is the translation of *Laxdaela Saga* by Muriel A.C. Press (London, 1899, J.M. Dent & Co.). William Morris made this saga known to readers of English poetry by his magnificent "Lovers of Gudrun." Mrs. Press lets us see the story in its original form. Perhaps this translation will appeal as widely as any to those who read, and we may note the differences between this form of writing and that to which the modern times are accustomed.

This saga is a story, but it is not like the work of fiction, nor like the sketch of history which appeals to our interest to-day. It has not the unity of purpose which marks the novel, nor the broad outlook over events which characterizes the history. Plotting is abundant, but plot in the technical sense there is none. Events are recorded in chronological order, but there is no march of those events to a *denouement*. While it would be wrong to say that there is no one hero in a saga, it would be more correct to say that that hero's name is legion. From generation to generation a saga-history wends its way, each period dominated by a great hero. The annals of a family edited for purposes of oral recitation, or the life of the principal member of that family with an introduction dealing with the great deeds of as many of his ancestors as he would be proud to own--this seems to be what a saga was--*Laxdaela*, *Grettla*, *Njala*.

This form permits many sterling literary qualities. Movement is the most marked characteristic. This was essential to a spoken story, and the sharpest impression left in the mind of an English reader is that of relentless activity. Thus he finds it necessary to keep the bearings of the story by consulting the list of *dramatis personae* and the map, both indispensable accompaniments of a saga-translation. The chapter headings make this list, and a glance at them for *Laxdaela* reveals a procession of notable personages--Ketill, Unn, Hoskuld, Olaf the Peacock, Kiartan, Gudrun, Bolli, Thorgills, Thorkell, Thorleik, Bolli Bollison and Snorri. Each of these is, in turn, the center of action, and only Gudrun keeps prominent for any length of time.

Character-portraiture, ever a remarkable achievement in literature, is excellently done in the sagas. There was a necessity for this; so many personages crowded the stage that, if they were not to be mere puppets, they would have to be carefully discriminated. That they were so a perusal of any saga will prove.

In a novel love is almost indispensable; in a saga other forces are the impelling motives. Love-making gets the novelist's tenderest interest and solicitude, but it receives little attention from the sagaman. Wooing under the Arctic Circle was a methodical bargaining, and there was little room for sentiment. When Thorvald asked for Osvif's daughter Gudrun, the father "said that against the match it would tell that he and Gudrun were not of equal standing. Thorvald spoke gently and said he was wooing a wife, not money. After that Gudrun was betrothed to Thorvald.... He should also bring her jewels, so that no woman of equal wealth should have better to show.... Gudrun was not asked about it and took it much to heart, yet things went on quietly." (Chap. XXXIV of **Laxdaela**.) In Iceland, as elsewhere, love was a source of discord, and for that reason love is always present in the saga. It is not the tender passion there, silvered with moonlight and attended by song. The saga is a man's tale.

The translation just referred to is in **The Temple Classics**, published by J.M. Dent & Co., London, 1899, and edited by Israel Gollancz. The editor promises (p. 273) other sagas in this form, if Mrs. Press's work prove successful. He speaks of **Njala** and **Volsunga** as imminent. It is to be hoped that the intention is to give the Dasent and the Morris versions, for they cannot be excelled.

Notes:

[Note 1: Quoted in Gray, by E.W. Gosse, English Men of Letters, p. 163.]

[Note 2: B. Hoff. Hovedpunkter af den Oldislandske litteratur-historie. Kobenhavn. 1873.]

[Note 3: Pp. xli-l in Selections from the Poetry and Prose of Thomas Gray, edited by W.L. Phelps. Ginn & Co., Boston. 1894.]

[Note 4: Life of Gray, pp. 160 ff.]

[Note 5: Wm. Sharp in Lyra Celtica, p. xx. Patrick Geddes and Colleagues. Edinburgh. 1896.]

[Note 6: Of Heroic Virtue, p. 355, Vol. III of Sir William Temple's Works. London. 1770.]

[Note 7: Of Heroic Virtue, p. 356.]

[Note 8: Of Poetry, p. 416.]

[Note 9: Spelling and punctuation are as in the original.]

[Note 10: Stopford Brooke, English Literature. D. Appleton & Co., New York. 1884. p. 150.]

[Note 11: Vol. 3, pp. 146-311.]

[Note 12: Quoted in Introduction, p. vii.]

[Note 13: Memoirs of the Life of Sir Walter Scott, Bart., Vol. I, p. 231. Boston, Houghton, Osgood & Co. 1879.]

[Note 14: Edinburgh Review, Oct., 1806.]

[Note 15: Quoted in Lockhart's Life, Vol. III, p. 241.]

[Note 16: In G.W. Dasent's Life of Cleasby, prefixed to the Icelandic-English Dictionary. Based on the MS. collection of the late Richard Cleasby, enlarged and completed by Gudbrand Vigfusson. Oxford.
1874.]

[Note 17: In another work by Carlyle, *The Early Kings of Norway* (1875) he takes special delight in revealing to Englishmen name etymologies that hark back to Norse times. Of this sort are Osborn from Osbjorn; Tooley St. (London) from St. Olave, St. Oley, Stooley, Tooley, (Chap. X).]

[Note 18: *The Early Kings of Norway* bears a later date--1875--than the works we are considering just now, and it is dealt with here only because Carlyle's **Heroes and Hero-Worship** belongs in the decade we are

considering.]

[Note 19: Chap. V of Preliminary Dissertation.]

[Note 20: Letters, Vol. I, p. 55, dated Dec. 12, 1855.]

[Note 21: Home of the Eddic Poems, p. xxxix. London, 1899. David Nutt.]

[Note 22: Introduction to the Cleasby Dictionary.]

[Note 23: Oxford Essays, 1858, p. 214.]

[Note 24: Lectures delivered in America in 1874, by Charles Kingsley. London. 1875. p. 71.]

[Note 25: P. 78.]

[Note 26: P. 89.]

[Note 27: P. 90.]

[Note 28: P. 91.]

[Note 29: P. 96.]

[Note 30: The Life of William Morris, by J.W. Mackail. London, New York, Bombay. Vol. I, p. 200.]

[Note 31: Edmond Scherer. Essays on English Literature, p. 309.]

[Note 32: Citations are from the 3d edition. Boston. 1881.]

[Note 33: Preface to Vol. I, p. v.]

[Note 34: The Wooing of Hallbiorn.]

The Codes Of Hammurabi And Moses
W. W. Davies

QTY

The discovery of the Hammurabi Code is one of the greatest achievements of archaeology, and is of paramount interest, not only to the student of the Bible, but also to all those interested in ancient history...

Religion   **ISBN:** *1-59462-338-4*   **Pages:132**
                                                 MSRP $12.95

The Theory of Moral Sentiments
Adam Smith

QTY

This work from 1749. contains original theories of con-science amd moral judgment and it is the foundation for systemof morals.

Philosophy **ISBN:** *1-59462-777-0*   **Pages:536**
                                                 MSRP $19.95

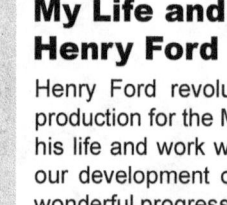

Jessica's First Prayer
Hesba Stretton

QTY

In a screened and secluded corner of one of the many railway-bridges which span the streets of London there could be seen a few years ago, from five o'clock every morning until half past eight, a tidily set-out coffee-stall, consisting of a trestle and board, upon which stood two large tin cans, with a small fire of charcoal burning under each so as to keep the coffee boiling during the early hours of the morning when the work-people were thronging into the city on their way to their daily toil...

Pages:84

Childrens   **ISBN:** *1-59462-373-2*   *MSRP $9.95*

My Life and Work
Henry Ford

QTY

Henry Ford revolutionized the world with his implementation of mass production for the Model T automobile. Gain valuable business insight into his life and work with his own auto-biography... "We have only started on our development of our country we have not as yet, with all our talk of wonderful progress, done more than scratch the surface. The progress has been wonderful enough but..."

Pages:300

Biographies/ **ISBN:** *1-59462-198-5*   *MSRP $21.95*

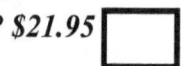

The Art of Cross-Examination
Francis Wellman

QTY

I presume it is the experience of every author, after his first book is published upon an important subject, to be almost overwhelmed with a wealth of ideas and illustrations which could readily have been included in his book, and which to his own mind, at least, seem to make a second edition inevitable. Such certainly was the case with me; and when the first edition had reached its sixth impression in five months, I rejoiced to learn that it seemed to my publishers that the book had met with a sufficiently favorable reception to justify a second and considerably enlarged edition. ..

Reference   **ISBN:** *1-59462-647-2*

Pages:412

MSRP $19.95

On the Duty of Civil Disobedience
Henry David Thoreau

QTY

Thoreau wrote his famous essay, On the Duty of Civil Disobedience, as a protest against an unjust but popular war and the immoral but popular institution of slave-owning. He did more than write—he declined to pay his taxes, and was hauled off to gaol in consequence. Who can say how much this refusal of his hastened the end of the war and of slavery ?

Law   **ISBN:** *1-59462-747-9*

Pages:48

MSRP $7.45

Dream Psychology Psychoanalysis for Beginners
Sigmund Freud

QTY

Sigmund Freud, born Sigismund Schlomo Freud (May 6, 1856 - September 23, 1939), was a Jewish-Austrian neurologist and psychiatrist who co-founded the psychoanalytic school of psychology. Freud is best known for his theories of the unconscious mind, especially involving the mechanism of repression; his redefinition of sexual desire as mobile and directed towards a wide variety of objects; and his therapeutic techniques, especially his understanding of transference in the therapeutic relationship and the presumed value of dreams as sources of insight into unconscious desires.

Psychology   **ISBN:** *1-59462-905-6*

Pages:196

MSRP $15.45

The Miracle of Right Thought
Orison Swett Marden

QTY

Believe with all of your heart that you will do what you were made to do. When the mind has once formed the habit of holding cheerful, happy, prosperous pictures, it will not be easy to form the opposite habit. It does not matter how improbable or how far away this realization may see, or how dark the prospects may be, if we visualize them as best we can, as vividly as possible, hold tenaciously to them and vigorously struggle to attain them, they will gradually become actualized, realized in the life. But a desire, a longing without endeavor, a yearning abandoned or held indifferently will vanish without realization.

Self Help   **ISBN:** *1-59462-644-8*

Pages:360

MSRP $25.45

QTY

The Rosicrucian Cosmo-Conception Mystic Christianity *by Max Heindel*   ISBN: *1-59462-188-8*   **$38.95**
The Rosicrucian Cosmo-conception is not dogmatic, neither does it appeal to any other authority than the reason of the student. It is: not controversial, but is: sent forth in the, hope that it may help to clear...   New Age/Religion Pages 646

Abandonment To Divine Providence *by Jean-Pierre de Caussade*   ISBN: *1-59462-228-0*   **$25.95**
"The Rev. Jean Pierre de Caussade was one of the most remarkable spiritual writers of the Society of Jesus in France in the 18th Century. His death took place at Toulouse in 1751. His works have gone through many editions and have been republished...   Inspirational/Religion Pages 400

Mental Chemistry *by Charles Haanel*   ISBN: *1-59462-192-6*   **$23.95**
Mental Chemistry allows the change of material conditions by combining and appropriately utilizing the power of the mind. Much like applied chemistry creates something new and unique out of careful combinations of chemicals the mastery of mental chemistry...   New Age Pages 354

The Letters of Robert Browning and Elizabeth Barret Barrett 1845-1846 vol II   ISBN: *1-59462-193-4*   **$35.95**
by Robert Browning and Elizabeth Barrett   Biographies Pages 596

Gleanings In Genesis (volume I) *by Arthur W. Pink*   ISBN: *1-59462-130-6*   **$27.45**
Appropriately has Genesis been termed "the seed plot of the Bible" for in it we have, in germ form, almost all of the great doctrines which are afterwards fully developed in the books of Scripture which follow...   Religion/Inspirational Pages 420

The Master Key *by L. W. de Laurence*   ISBN: *1-59462-001-6*   **$30.95**
In no branch of human knowledge has there been a more lively increase of the spirit of research during the past few years than in the study of Psychology, Concentration and Mental Discipline. The requests for authentic lessons in Thought Control, Mental Discipline and...   New Age/Business Pages 422

The Lesser Key Of Solomon Goetia *by L. W. de Laurence*   ISBN: *1-59462-092-X*   **$9.95**
This translation of the first book of the "Lemegton" which is now for the first time made accessible to students of Talismanic Magic was done, after careful collation and edition, from numerous Ancient Manuscripts in Hebrew, Latin, and French...   New Age/Occult Pages 92

Rubaiyat Of Omar Khayyam *by Edward Fitzgerald*   ISBN:*1-59462-332-5*   **$13.95**
Edward Fitzgerald, whom the world has already learned, in spite of his own efforts to remain within the shadow of anonymity, to look upon as one of the rarest poets of the century, was born at Bredfield, in Suffolk, on the 31st of March, 1809. He was the third son of John Purcell...   Music Pages 172

Ancient Law *by Henry Maine*   ISBN: *1-59462-128-4*   **$29.95**
The chief object of the following pages is to indicate some of the earliest ideas of mankind, as they are reflected in Ancient Law, and to point out the relation of those ideas to modern thought.   Religiom/History Pages 452

Far-Away Stories *by William J. Locke*   ISBN: *1-59462-129-2*   **$19.45**
"Good wine needs no bush, but a collection of mixed vintages does. And this book is just such a collection. Some of the stories I do not want to remain buried for ever in the museum files of dead magazine-numbers an author's not unpardonable vanity..."   Fiction Pages 272

Life of David Crockett *by David Crockett*   ISBN: *1-59462-250-7*   **$27.45**
"Colonel David Crockett was one of the most remarkable men of the times in which he lived. Born in humble life, but gifted with a strong will, an indomitable courage, and unremitting perseverance...   Biographies/New Age Pages 424

Lip-Reading *by Edward Nitchie*   ISBN: *1-59462-206-X*   **$25.95**
Edward B. Nitchie, founder of the New York School for the Hard of Hearing, now the Nitchie School of Lip-Reading, Inc, wrote "LIP-READING Principles and Practice". The development and perfecting of this meritorious work on lip-reading was an undertaking...   How-to Pages 400

A Handbook of Suggestive Therapeutics, Applied Hypnotism, Psychic Science   ISBN: *1-59462-214-0*   **$24.95**
by Henry Munro   Health/New Age/Health/Self-help Pages 376

A Doll's House: and Two Other Plays *by Henrik Ibsen*   ISBN: *1-59462-112-8*   **$19.95**
Henrik Ibsen created this classic when in revolutionary 1848 Rome. Introducing some striking concepts in playwriting for the realist genre, this play has been studied the world over.   Fiction/Classics/Plays 308

The Light of Asia *by sir Edwin Arnold*   ISBN: *1-59462-204-3*   **$13.95**
In this poetic masterpiece, Edwin Arnold describes the life and teachings of Buddha. The man who was to become known as Buddha to the world was born as Prince Gautama of India but he rejected the worldly riches and abandoned the reigns of power when...   Religion/History/Biographies Pages 170

The Complete Works of Guy de Maupassant *by Guy de Maupassant*   ISBN: *1-59462-157-8*   **$16.95**
"For days and days, nights and nights, I had dreamed of that first kiss which was to consecrate our engagement, and I knew not on what spot I should put my lips..."   Fiction/Classics Pages 240

The Art of Cross-Examination *by Francis L. Wellman*   ISBN: *1-59462-309-0*   **$26.95**
Written by a renowned trial lawyer, Wellman imparts his experience and uses case studies to explain how to use psychology to extract desired information through questioning.   How-to/Science/Reference Pages 408

Answered or Unanswered? *by Louisa Vaughan*   ISBN: *1-59462-248-5*   **$10.95**
Miracles of Faith in China   Religion Pages 112

The Edinburgh Lectures on Mental Science (1909) *by Thomas*   ISBN: *1-59462-008-3*   **$11.95**
This book contains the substance of a course of lectures recently given by the writer in the Queen Street Hail, Edinburgh. Its purpose is to indicate the Natural Principles governing the relation between Mental Action and Material Conditions...   New Age/Psychology Pages 148

Ayesha *by H. Rider Haggard*   ISBN: *1-59462-301-5*   **$24.95**
Verily and indeed it is the unexpected that happens! Probably if there was one person upon the earth from whom the Editor of this, and of a certain previous history, did not expect to hear again...   Classics Pages 380

Ayala's Angel *by Anthony Trollope*   ISBN: *1-59462-352-X*   **$29.95**
The two girls were both pretty, but Lucy who was twenty-one who supposed to be simple and comparatively unattractive, whereas Ayala was credited, as her Bombwhat romantic name might show, with poetic charm and a taste for romance. Ayala when her father died was nineteen...   Fiction Pages 484

The American Commonwealth *by James Bryce*   ISBN: *1-59462-286-8*   **$34.45**
An interpretation of American democratic political theory. It examines political mechanics and society from the perspective of Scotsman James Bryce   Politics Pages 572

Stories of the Pilgrims *by Margaret P. Pumphrey*   ISBN: *1-59462-116-0*   **$17.95**
This book explores pilgrims religious oppression in England as well as their escape to Holland and eventual crossing to America on the Mayflower, and their early days in New England...   History Pages 268

QTY

The Fasting Cure *by Sinclair Upton* ISBN: *1-59462-222-1* **$13.95**
In the Cosmopolitan Magazine for May, 1910, and in the Contemporary Review (London) for April, 1910, I published an article dealing with my experiences in fasting. I have written a great many magazine articles, but never one which attracted so much attention... New Age/Self Help/Health Pages 164

Hebrew Astrology *by Sepharial* ISBN: *1-59462-308-2* **$13.45**
In these days of advanced thinking it is a matter of common observation that we have left many of the old landmarks behind and that we are now pressing forward to greater heights and to a wider horizon than that which represented the mind-content of our progenitors... Astrology Pages 144

Thought Vibration or The Law of Attraction in the Thought World ISBN: *1-59462-127-6* **$12.95**
by William Walker Atkinson *Psychology/Religion Pages 144*

Optimism *by Helen Keller* ISBN: *1-59462-108-X* **$15.95**
Helen Keller was blind, deaf, and mute since 19 months old, yet famously learned how to overcome these handicaps, communicate with the world, and spread her lectures promoting optimism. An inspiring read for everyone... Biographies/Inspirational Pages 84

Sara Crewe *by Frances Burnett* ISBN: *1-59462-360-0* **$9.45**
In the first place, Miss Minchin lived in London. Her home was a large, dull, tall one, in a large, dull square, where all the houses were alike, and all the sparrows were alike, and where all the door-knockers made the same heavy sound... Childrens/Classic Pages 88

The Autobiography of Benjamin Franklin *by Benjamin Franklin* ISBN: *1-59462-135-7* **$24.95**
The Autobiography of Benjamin Franklin has probably been more extensively read than any other American historical work, and no other book of its kind has had such ups and downs of fortune. Franklin lived for many years in England, where he was agent... Biographies/History Pages 332

Name	
Email	
Telephone	
Address	
City, State ZIP	

☐ **Credit Card**   ☐ **Check / Money Order**

Credit Card Number	
Expiration Date	
Signature	

Please Mail to: Book Jungle
                    PO Box 2226
                    Champaign, IL 61825
or Fax to: 630-214-0564

ORDERING INFORMATION

web: *www.bookjungle.com*
email: *sales@bookjungle.com*
fax: *630-214-0564*
mail: *Book Jungle PO Box 2226 Champaign, IL 61825*
or PayPal *to sales@bookjungle.com*

Please contact us for bulk discounts

DIRECT-ORDER TERMS

**20% Discount if You Order
Two or More Books**
Free Domestic Shipping!
Accepted: Master Card, Visa,
Discover, American Express